D0350240

BLACK ALLEY

MICKEY SPILLANE

BLACK ALLEY

A DUTTON BOOK

DUTTON

Published by the Penguin Group
Penguin Books USA Inc., 375 Hudson Street, New York, New York 10014, U.S.A.
Penguin Books Ltd, 27 Wrights Lane, London W8 5TZ, England
Penguin Books Australia Ltd, Ringwood, Victoria, Australia
Penguin Books Canada Ltd, 10 Alcorn Avenue, Toronto, Ontario, Canada M4V 3B2
Penguin Books (N.Z.) Ltd, 182–190 Wairau Road, Auckland 10, New Zealand

Penguin Books Ltd, Registered Offices:
Harmondsworth, Middlesex, England

First published by Dutton, an imprint of Dutton Signet,
a division of Penguin Books USA Inc.
Distributed in Canada by McClelland & Stewart Inc.

First Printing, November, 1996
10 9 8 7 6 5 4 3 2 1

REGISTERED TRADEMARK—MARCA REGISTRADA

Library of Congress Cataloging-in-Publication-Data:

Spillane, Mickey
Black Alley/Mickey Spillane.
p. cm.
ISBN 0-525-94229-7
1. Hammer, Mike (Fictitious character)—Fiction. 2. Private investigators—United States—Fiction. I. Title.
PS3537.P652B57 1996
813'.54—dc20 96-15952
CIP

Printed in the United States of America
Set in New Baskerville

Designed by Jesse Cohen

PUBLISHER'S NOTE
This is a work of fiction. Names, characters, places, and incidents either are the products of the author's imagination or are used fictitiously, and any resemblance to actual persons, living or dead, events, or locales is entirely coincidental.

This book is printed on acid-free paper. ♾

This is for Max Allan Collins, who prowled the BLACK ALLEYS with Dick Tracy. Now he has to do it by himself.

1

THE PHONE RANG.

It was a thing that had been sitting here, black and quiet like a holstered gun, unlisted, unknown to anybody, used only for local outgoing calls, and when it was triggered it had the soft, muted sound of a silenced automatic. The first ring was a warning round. The second time would be death calling.

Eight months ago I had come to Florida to die. The two bullets I had caught in the firefight under the West Side Drive had churned into bodily areas that weren't made to be violated like that and the blood that had spilled out of me was just too much, so the others, the walking wounded and the repairable, were taken care of first by the few medics who got to the battleground early. The dead and dying were pushed aside or isolated in the section of no return.

The temperature was six below zero and it kept me from dying on the spot because the blood coagulated and clotted in ugly smears of cloth and skin and the pain hadn't started yet, so when the little fat guy who saw my eyes open and still bright pulled me away from the carnage he was almost in the shock I was going into. Nobody would listen to him. He was a drunk. I was nearly dead.

Sometimes the body responds to a stimulus that can't be explained. He got me upright. I walked woodenly, dyingly. I was sat in an old car. The fat man rolled down the windows. The blood stayed frozen. My hands were numb and I couldn't feel my feet. Idly, I wondered what frostbite was like. Breathing was a thing that was happening, but at a pace that said it could slow, then stop at any time. A dull, squeezing sensation of pain was beginning to gnaw on my insides and I knew that eventually, and very soon, it would grow into a terrible, devastating animal with an awful hunger and I would be eaten alive by it.

I wanted to scream, but nothing would come out.

Every minute it got worse.

Then there was nothing, but I didn't know that.

When the light came back it was soft and the things in it were a little blurry, fuzzy and shadowy, so I closed my eyes and opened them again after a few moments and the things began to take recognizable shape. There were hands and arms, then a face I didn't know, an old face with white hair whose countenance was frowning and concerned, whose hands were busy doing things to my body and by the feel and the smell I knew were changing the bandages.

He saw me looking at him and said, "Don't talk."

I had been around too long to be overly curious about this *BIG NOW* that had happened to me. I knew it was bad. I didn't talk. He read my answer in my eyes and nodded.

When he finished with the bandage he pulled the sheet

up over my chest and fingered his glasses down on his nose so that our eyes met directly. "I'll ask you questions," he said. "Don't try to answer them. Just blink once for yes and twice for no. Can you do that?"

For a moment I let it sink in, then I blinked once.

"Do you know what happened to you?"

I blinked again.

He pinched his nose between his thumb and forefinger. "You should be dead, you know." There was no answer to that.

The eerie swirling in my eyesight cleared up, and I saw the little fat man, only he wasn't the same little fat man that had dragged me from dull red-smeared concrete where sirens and screams blended into a death opera beyond imagination.

"For the past fifteen days you've been here."

I just looked at him. He was in white now, jacket, pants, and he had a stethoscope hung from his neck. He knew what I was thinking.

"I used to be a doctor." He frowned again and pinched his nose tighter. "Wrong word," he said. "I still *am* a doctor. I was never kicked out of the profession. I just left. I got drunk and left. Period. I couldn't stand the crap."

There were no blinks to tell him what I wanted to know. *Yes* and *No* just wouldn't do it so all I could do was stare and hope he could read what was back there.

He did.

"Where I was, nobody cared. The ideals of youth went down the drain during internship. Man, did they go down the drain." He took a deep breath and grimaced. "For thirty years I went into the system. Man, I got rich." He leaned forward, closer to my face. "Do I look rich to you?"

This time I blinked twice. No.

Somehow, the circuitry of my mind began functioning

and I was hoping that I wasn't being smothered by some kind of a nutcase who wanted to play a game of *you die* on his own fiddle. I tried to move my arms and they moved. My fingers wiggled, my shoulders were free. There were no restraints. But the bonds were still there. Total weakness still had me; restraints or not, there was little I could do.

Very professionally, he reached down, wrapped his fingers around my wrist and took my pulse. He didn't look at his watch. He didn't have any. "Before you get too choked up, kiddo, I can do this by heart. I hocked the Rolex years ago," he told me.

I blinked four times to show that I understood.

"You hurt?" he asked.

I tried a shrug with my face.

"At least you don't feel anything too bad, right?"

I blinked.

"Good. So I'll talk and you listen. Maybe I can make a story out of this. It's got a great beginning. I wish I knew the ending. You ready?"

For a long second I wondered, then knew it was a must. I was alive. Why? *Once more I blinked.*

He ran his hands across his face, gathering his thoughts. They weren't just idle bits and pieces he was trying to put into place. It was like the closing of a bridge across a great river; he was putting the roadway back in line and was about to drive his car across it. What he was about to say was scaring him, but it had to be said or he'd never cross the bridge.

"I walked out of a hospital here in New York and right into a saloon. In less than a month a fine surgeon disintegrated into a total alcoholic with no regrets, no remorse, no aches and pains. My money-hungry family just let me go, took all the assets and never even bothered to report me to the Missing Persons Bureau. After seven years I was declared legally dead, my wife got a young stud to take her to bed, my kids went to pot, to coke and to poverty and all this I found out in the newspapers. Great system, isn't it?"

I didn't blink this time either. He wasn't done with the story.

"You feel tired, blink three times and I'll shut up," he said.

I blinked *yes.*

"The night of the shooting," he told me, "I was in Casey's saloon. A dive. I had been there plenty of times. It was all I could afford. I had one buck and a dime left and was half drunk. That's when the shooting began. You know, I don't even remember running outside. All of a sudden I was there. Hell, I didn't know what was going on, all those cars and the sirens. Everybody was yelling and everyplace people were making the dead sounds and I started to get sick to my stomach. When I saw that guy drag you off that wooden case and just drop you there . . . well, whatever I had been came back to me and I pulled you over to my car."

My eyes squinted at him and he nodded. "That buggy was twelve years old. It was all I had left. I stole license plates to keep it current. I took you back here."

This time I let my eyes pass around the room. I was able to see more clearly now.

Understanding, he said: "Tools of my trade. Some things you can never get rid of." He grinned and looked around the room himself. "Man, this is right out of *Gunsmoke.* You and old doc, no modern goodies, no big antibiotics, just a booze tranquilizer, a few instruments and a lot of hope." Once more, he got that furrow between his brows. "You should be dead, you know that?"

One quick blink. Yes, I know that. Maybe I still will be.

Almost apologetically, he said, "Everything I could do, I did."

This time I didn't blink at all. I was waiting.

"I was drunk and I had the shakes." He watched me closely, but I didn't respond. *No blinks.* "It was like something dropped you right into my lap. I was being given another chance. What I did was totally unethical, completely unwise. When I should have taken you to a hospital to receive proper care, I took the responsibility upon myself like a complete fool, and by some happy circumstance, you survived all the indignities of a medical idiot and stayed alive in spite of what he did."

That stupid blinking was beginning to bother me. It hurt, but I breathed in a little deeper and said in a strange voice, "Would I have lived otherwise?"

His lips pursed and his eyes grew oddly serious. "No," he said. Then added, "You almost went down the black alley. Nobody comes back from there."

I remembered it then. The street I was on was strange, yet one I knew. A dim light was on either end, but I was in the middle, and something was there in front and behind that I didn't want to face. Right beside me was an opening. It went somewhere. No . . . it went nowhere, but it was a way to escape the street. It looked cool and comfortable, an alley I could be safe in. It was black.

And black had a meaning. It wasn't death. Black didn't represent death no matter what they told you. Grey represented death. Black was the color of ignorance.

So I stood there and looked down the black alley and didn't step into it. I just melted back into a bubbly froth of anesthesia make-believe and awoke to a blurry fat man's face.

I said, "Am I . . . dying?" My voice was cobwebby, shaky.

Finally, he told me, "That's up to you now." I saw a

small smile touch his mouth and he added, "Just don't do it. If you die, you kill me, too. Lousy choice for both of us."

He saw the question in my eyes.

"Why? Man, if you kick it over in my home-made laboratory here I'm right down the drain. A month ago I wouldn't have given a hoot. Hell, I would have welcomed the *big out.* Then you go and show up all blown to pieces and I take the challenge and make it real again, suddenly turning into a doctor who pulled off some kind of a modern miracle . . . and if you go, I'm right behind you."

I had to force the words out. "Now you're . . . sober?"

"Permanently."

I was trying to verbalize another thought, but he held up his hand and shook his head at the same time. "No more talking." He reached over to the table beside the bed and picked up a hypodermic needle. He shook some alcohol on a cotton swab, dabbed my arm and gave me a jab. "Just some sleep, no black alley this time."

Somehow my mind had kept a count and I knew four more days had passed. In a way I had been fed with the life-sustaining solutions that pass through tubes into your veins and nourish the body, and the same body had been moved and massaged so that no muscular deterioration would set in and wet cloths had kept the skin clean.

Then I woke up and there was no fuzziness at all. The soft light of dawn made everything a dull cream color and I was able to breathe without it hurting at all. The door opened and the little fat man was there again. He didn't seem so fat now. There was a drawn look to his face that was an improvement.

I think I grinned at him.

"You feel better?" he asked me.

I made the *okay* sign with my fingers and blinked *yes.*

"Cut out the blinking, friend. I think you can try speaking to me. What do you want to know?"

"How much do I owe you?" I said. My voice was there, but deep and raspy.

He dropped his head and let out a grunt. His eyes lifted to mine. "Joking?"

"Sure."

"Otherwise I'd have to tell you that I owed you," he said. After a moment he added, "I still might. If you want to take me to court you'd own my hide."

"Knock it off," I let out softly. "I'm alive."

"I think that was your doing, not mine."

"Don't give me that."

"I have to. Right now you're on the upswing. There's no way you're going to come out of this like you had a broken leg or the mumps or something. You are in a very trepidatious situation." He squinted and ran his hand across his face. "Damn, what a bedside manner I have. I shouldn't even be talking to you like this."

"Hey . . ."

"You like the rough news?"

I nodded.

"There's nothing I can do for you anymore. If you want to keep functioning you are going to have to get rest so damn complete it will drive you crazy." He stopped, wiped his mouth, then continued. "And I *mean* rest. Doing nothing. Taking it easy. Getting up, napping, going to bed early, just like some little preschool kid. That's the only way your insides are ever going to come together and start working again."

"For how long?"

He let a few seconds pass, then said, "You'll know."

"Will I ever be the same?"

"You'll know that too when the time comes."

He kept looking at me, not wanting to put his thoughts into words. I got tired of waiting and asked, "What's missing, doc?"

"You just sounded like Bugs Bunny."

"Cut the comedy."

"Sure." He licked his lips and a darkness came into his eyes. "I just found out who you are."

I waited.

"A private investigator." I didn't have to blink on that one. He knew. "Mike Hammer."

"Right. Is that bad?"

"No. Just trouble."

"Why?"

"You are supposed to be dead." He read the expression on my face and said, "Witnesses saw you shot. You were right near the pilings on the wharf. They said you were trying to get up and assumed you did and fell into the river."

He was trying to get his composure so I kept quiet. When he could speak again he said, "It was a full moon, the tide was going out fast and anything or anybody in the river at the time would have been swept out to sea. There was a search off the docks and at the mouth of the Hudson but nothing was recovered."

"Naturally," I told him.

"Don't get smart, Mr. Hammer."

"Sorry."

"Until now I didn't know the attention you'd get from the press. They don't know whether to treat your demise as a loss or a gain to society."

"What do you think?"

He picked up my arm and felt my pulse again, a medical pause for thought. When a full minute had passed he let my hand drop and said, "As a doctor, I'm only concerned about your getting better."

"That's not what you're thinking."

"You really a killer, Mike?" he asked suddenly and bluntly.

"Not the kind you have in mind."

"What kind are there?"

"Legal," I said. "Illegal."

"Explain."

"Kill your enemy on the street, the chair. The rope. The lethal injection. Kill your enemy in war, the medal, the honor, the reward."

"Which were you, Mike?"

I grinned at him. I let him see my teeth in the grin because I had been there and he hadn't. He never knew the necessity of inflicting death or the pain that it caused. He never knew who it hurt the most or what he would have done in the same circumstances.

No blinking at all now. I said, "As a doctor, does it really matter to you?" He scowled at me. "Would you keep a patient healthy so he could be executed?"

"Tough question, kid."

"Would you?"

"Yes."

"Why?"

"I took an oath."

"Horse manure." I started to breathe a little hard and let myself fall back on the pillow. He just let me lie there until I had settled down, then wiped my face with a wet towel. There was a hotness under my skin and a tingling sensation was beginning to run up my arms. Suddenly I could feel the sweat starting and there was that short prick in my upper arm from a needle and I relaxed into another sleep.

* * *

I was his project. There was nothing I could do on my own except stay alive and let all the pieces come back together. If it happened, then he would become whole again.

Years ago he had bought a place on the Florida Keys, a little south of Marathon on the west side, a concrete block building on a peninsula of land fronting on the Gulf with a thirty-foot-deep channel running along one side, a relic from when the state had needed the coquina to lay a roadbed to Key West.

It was quiet. I was alone. I had the papers, a TV, a radio with AM and FM, and if I wanted to listen to the boat traffic, a VHF because we bordered on the Gulf and it was allowed. There was a base station for CB traffic if I wanted to hear the truckers on Route 1 or the kids making dates for some key-hopping.

The papers were delivered every morning with the daily groceries and each day I faded from the news until I disappeared altogether. The doctor's name was Ralph Morgan and I wondered how he was handling all the details of the situation until I realized that death was a complete wipe-out and there was nothing to consider anymore.

Wednesday he drove up to the door. He was even thinner now, a new seriousness to him. He sat down and had a cold Miller Lite beer before he leaned back in the old chair and stared at me hard. "How do you feel?"

"I phone you the details every day."

"That's crap. How do you feel?"

"Physically?"

"Yes."

"I'll make it," I said.

"Don't give me that."

"You mean how is my psychological makeup?"

"Something like that."

"Lousy."

"Why?"

"Doctor," I said, "I'm alive, but out of life. It's something I have to get back into."

"Why?"

"How long can a person stay dead?" I asked him.

"If you go back, they'll kill you," he told me.

"You've been doing research, doctor."

"Not only on you, kiddo, but on me, too. I went down just as deep as you did. I'm absolutely scared out of my head. I'm a doctor, I want to *be* a doctor, and for the first time in years I know I *can be* a doctor. I pulled off the big surgical plus on you, but nobody will ever hear about it and if they do I'm a real shot-down MD."

"So what happens to me, doc?"

"You read the papers, didn't you?"

"Sure. It was one hell of a shootout. Two of the New York families decided to gun it when the big don was coming off the ship from a trip to the old country. It was completely idiotic. Everything was going smooth, no heat was on, the politicians were all in their pockets with the judges and the DA's, the press was quiet, then everything blew up in their faces."

"Why, Mike? You knew. You were there."

"My squeal was nothing. He heard the word and knew that I had that run-in with the don two months ago. Somebody was getting ready to knock him off as soon as he got back into this country and I was going to be set up for it."

"Then what were you doing there anyway?"

"It may sound pretty stupid, but I wanted to let the old man know he was going to be hit. I didn't want any contracts going out on me. That damn mob might be going nice and legitimate, but they have a long memory and longer arms. They got contacts and a communications web almost as good as the feds."

"What happened?"

"Don't ask me. Something went all out of focus. That old cargo ship was four hours late getting into port and the Gaetano bunch was waiting for them. When I drove up I didn't see any sign of an ambush at all and when it happened it was like they came out of the woodwork. Or the concrete. Very professional. Damn near military style."

"It was over in three minutes," Dr. Morgan blurted. "Both sides started shooting at the same time."

"You can bet the don kept himself covered. He would have his own guys on board and some others meeting the ship, too. He probably had them in place even before the others showed up."

"Come on, Mike, can you pull off a situation like that in a public place?"

I shook my head at his naïveté. "Two A.M. at the piers in New York City isn't exactly a public place these days. The don still has a heavy hand in union affairs around there and handpicking his guys for work duty as a cover would be no trouble at all."

"This . . . this *squeal* of yours say the don was coming out the office door instead of the main exit?"

"A few would come out first, then the don, and they'd hop into a car that was waiting for them. I had pulled up behind their limo and was getting out when the first shots went off. As far as I could tell, they came from the other area."

The doctor took a long pull of the beer and set the empty can down. For a few seconds he squinted, then ran his fingers through his thinning hair. "Did the Ponti kid see you . . . or recognize you before you shot him?"

"Are you kidding, doc? Sure he saw me, he was looking straight at me then *he shot me.* Oh, he knew what he was doing, all right. He caught me coming head-on and nailed me with that .357 he always packs. I went down on my back and half rolled over when he came up and pointed that rod right at my face, hating me so much he never saw the .45 I had in my fist and that was the end of Azi Ponti right there. I remembered hearing some of the firefight and being dragged along the street, but that was all."

Idly, Dr. Morgan reached over for the beer can and squashed it with his fingertips. "They used to make them stronger," he said.

"They were steel then. They didn't pollute. They'd rust away to nothing."

"Why do they use aluminum, then?"

"Because it's scarcer, it costs more and pollutes better."

"You can recycle aluminum."

"Only a fraction goes in the collection bins. Who wants to kill me?"

"I understand the don made several hard remarks about you. Trouble is, he'd have a hard time proving it." He saw the puzzled look on my face. "You never dropped your gun, Mike. You held onto it until I forced it out of your grasp while you were unconscious."

"Forget it, doc," I said. "Ballistics have matching slugs from my piece on file."

He shook his head slowly. "To match with what? The bullets that hit the Ponti kid penetrated and were never found. The police assume he was shot in the general fighting."

"That kind of information wasn't in the papers, doc."

"I know," he agreed. "I pulled a few medical strings that led to the autopsy report and there it is. I may have been a drunk, but that knowledge was only for the few intimate cronies I had in the saloon circle. They figured I was a drunk remittance man being paid to stay away from home. Or on social security. It bought them drinks so they couldn't care less."

"So I can go back then," I stated.

"Not yet." His tone was solemn. I waited a few seconds, knowing he'd start again. "Your prognosis is acceptable. In other words, you will live . . . IF."

A little of that cold fear touched my belly again. "Great," I said.

"Three months from now I may be able to give you a definite statement."

"You haven't said what the *IF* was."

He got up, walked to the cooler and slid another Miller Lite out of the ice. My mouth went dry and I could almost taste the brew, but any alcoholic beverage was on my forbidden list. He took a good taste, watching me, enjoying my discomfort. "It's pretty damn hot down here in Florida, kid."

"Come on, it's summertime, man."

He tilted the can again for a big swallow, then wiped his mouth with the back of his hand. "You stay exactly on the schedule I set for you. The prescribed regimen of diet is not to be changed. The exercise will take place as detailed, the medication as specified. If the routine is followed to its minutest specification, there is a good possibility that you will survive. Mess around with what I've laid out and you look smack at the big *IF*. You buy the farm. It's dead time."

"Your bedside manner gets worse all the time. You talk like me now."

"I just don't want to upset you," he told me with a sour grin. "Your only big point is your psychological outlook, Mike. Nothing seems to put a dent in that."

"How do you know so much about me?"

"You were big news."

"Were?"

He sat down and inched his chair forward, his arms propped on his knees. "You are presumed dead. Your good friend in the police department, Patrick Chambers, had a memorial service for you. The place was pretty well packed with an odd assortment of mourners."

"At least I didn't leave any clients hanging," I said. "My work file was pretty well cleaned up."

"Well, your secretary . . ."

"Velda?"

"Yes. She's going to keep your office open for now."

"She's got her own PI ticket. She can handle it."

Then, suddenly, I wasn't feeling good at all. I had a weightlessness, empty sensation and an odd faraway buzzing in my ears. I could feel an involuntary relaxation of my muscles, as if I were melting, and the doctor came out of his chair, felt my pulse and muttered something unintelligible and stretched me out on the floor.

I opened my eyes and he looked at me. "I was wrong, Mike. Something did put a dent in that mental outlook of yours."

My eyes closed and I lay there, trying to see what it was like to be dead.

It was lousy.

Cold wet towels wiped the sweat away from me and blew the life spark into a small flame, and when it was big enough the doctor asked, "You ready to sit up?"

One blink. Yes. Talking was a little too much trouble.

Between the two of us I got back to a seated position

and took deliberate breaths until I was normal again. "Was that episode bad, doc?"

"Not good, but not threatening. You feel okay?"

"Like a million," I told him.

"Sure."

I took a sip of ice water from the glass beside my chair. Just one small sip, that's all I was allowed. "I think we're both in the same boat, doc."

"Which one is that?"

"The one going up crap creek without a paddle."

"Oh?"

"We're both supposed to be dead. How do we go back?"

The first few weeks drifted by like some casual dream. The lethargy was chemically induced to make any physical action too difficult to bother with, and although my mind could register sight and sound and smells, it did it with an attitude of mild complacency, hardly attempting to record it on a memory circuit.

Some of it made humorous impressions . . . the doctor speaking to someone in banking and arranging for a money transfer. His buddies, the drunks, would really enjoy that one. A little part of me wanted to ask him how he squirreled money away when he left home. Those things could be done, but how? One time there was the gibberish of medical talk I couldn't understand. A box of pharmaceutical supplies came in the mail.

I woke up before the sun rose, the salt air of the Gulf blowing in the window smelling warm and lazy, with a slight fishy touch. This wasn't one of those unreal days at all. This was alive and had a texture to it. Then there was another familiar smell that came with a special appreciation because there was more to it than an aroma.

Dr. Morgan came in with a pot of steaming coffee and a fat white mug. "How do you like it?"

"Two Sweet 'N Lows. No milk."

"I had you figured for straight black."

"That's only for tough guys," I told him.

He opened his hand and had a few pink packets of the sweetener, dirty and wrinkled lying there. They looked like they had come out of the garbage pail. "Know where I got them?" I didn't bother to answer him. "They were in your coat pocket."

"Why'd you figure me black then?"

"Bad diagnosis. You want them?"

"Certainly."

The paper might have been messy, but the coffee tasted just right. It was the first cup I had had in a long time and I thought I'd be able to finish the whole pot, but halfway through the mug I put it down and looked dubiously at Dr. Morgan.

"No sweat," he said. "Your body's talking to you. Don't force yourself to take more than you need. Hungry?"

"Not really. That half cup of coffee filled me up."

"Later I'll get you into some normal groceries."

"How come you're being so nice to me?" I asked him.

Once more I got one of his concerned doctor frowns and he said, "You've turned a corner. Now you're entering a new phase."

"I didn't mean it that way," I said.

The frown turned into an embarrassed grin. "Well . . . no sense lying to you."

"So?"

"I need your expertise." He saw the expression on my face. "Your advice," he added.

"On what?"

"On how not to go to jail. I'm running around in the

old jalopy with stolen New York plates and sure as hell I'm going to get stopped because the wreck is smoking, the tires are bad and the muffler is making a racket."

It was nice to be needed. I didn't even have to think hard on that one. "You got any money, doc?"

"Yeah, I was never *that* much of a dummy."

"Got your old papers?"

"Whatever was in my wallet. Driver's license, an old voter registration, medical ID from the hospital, stuff like that."

"Great. Then go buy a car, get it legally registered in your right name, then get licensed in the state. You can prove your identity and just tell them that total retirement didn't suit you and you want back into the action if they ask you any questions."

"Mike, I am supposed to be *legally dead*!"

"Look, doc," I told him roughly, "who's going to remember a stupid action that took place so many years ago? Besides, you don't *look* dead at all. Believe me, nobody's going to bother you. Only first get yourself some decent clothes to make it all believable. Plaid pants, maybe, and a golf shirt with a lizard on it."

"I don't play golf."

"So get a fishing shirt."

He stood there looking down at me. Then he let out a big smile and said, "Man, I didn't enjoy being dead at all."

The phone rang. The doctor wasn't here to answer it. Whenever he did there was something of importance to be said, medical or household needs to be discussed.

I picked the receiver off the cradle and in as growling voice as I could put on, said, "Yes?"

When I heard his first word I felt a chill work its way across my shoulders. He said, "Hi, Mike, feeling better?"

His tone was as pleasant as could be, as though there had been no break at all in our relationship, no firefight on the dockside.

For a second I paused, took a breath, then said normally, "How'd you know where to find me, Pat?"

"I'm a cop, remember. Captains have a little clout."

"Where you calling from?"

"A safe phone in a closed booth in a department store."

"Then how'd you locate me?"

"It wasn't easy," he told me.

"Since you found me, somebody else can."

"Not unless they have the manpower and electronics we have," Pat said.

I took another deep, easy breath. "Then tell me this, pal. Why?"

This time he paused a moment. "Somebody shot Marcos Dooley."

Softly, I muttered, "Damn."

Pat knew what I was thinking and let me take my time. Old buddy Marcos Dooley had brought Pat and me into the intelligence end of the military before the war ended and steered us to where we were today. Only Pat could still wear the uniform, an NYPD blue. I carried a New York State PI ticket and a permit to keep a concealed weapon on my person. Marcos Dooley had become a wild-ass bum, and now he was dead. But we had backed each other up during the raging times of hot shrapnel and bullets that sang high-pitched songs of destruction, and we had beaten the death game because we'd done it right and covered each other's tails until our hearts stopped pounding and breathing became easier.

"What happened, Pat?"

"Somebody broke into the house and shot him in the guts."

"You know who?"

"Not yet. We *may* have a suspect."

"Anyone I know?"

"Sure. You shot his brother. Ugo Ponti."

I said something unintelligible. "How is he?"

"Dying. Do you think you can make it up here? He wants to see you."

"I'll be there." Then I added, "How's Velda, Pat?"

I knew he was grinning into the phone. "Waiting," he told me. "She never could see you dying."

The doctor had gotten me an early flight into New York and had sprung for a first-class ticket to give me plenty of room to stretch out and rest. I told the stewardess not to awaken me until we were in the traffic pattern, then kicked off my loafers and went to sleep. There were no narcotics this time. It was pure, natural sleep with unnatural dreams so disturbingly real they twisted me back to wakefulness just to get rid of them. Faces were distorted, yet ones I knew, and the dream sounds made banging noises that came out of a past I didn't want to remember. Somehow time compacted itself and before I could swing at the thing that had grabbed me I opened my eyes and saw the pretty stewardess shaking me awake very gently and made myself smile.

But she knew. "Bad dreams?"

"Terrible," I told her.

"You wanted to clobber me, didn't you?"

"Not you."

"Who then?"

"The bad guys," I said.

"You military?"

"A long time ago."

"Now you're a cop." The tiny frown between her eyes had a smile to it.

"Of a sort," I said.

The frown went away but the smile stayed. "Ohooo," she said, "one of those." She saw that I was wondering what she was getting at and added, "A terrorist, like."

This time I grinned and straightened up, bringing the seat back to an upright position as the PA directed. I said, "You might say that."

The smile I got back said she didn't believe me at all.

It was off season for the return of the snowbirds to the big city so there weren't many there to meet the passengers. I slung the single piece of luggage over my shoulder and ambled slowly down the corridor, walking too slowly to be a native New Yorker. Everybody else from the plane passed me by before I reached the gate and that strange thrill of anticipation ran up my spine before I ever spotted Pat Chambers and Velda watching me, not really knowing what to expect, a walking dead man, a ghost from the past, or somebody with a crazy, writhing anger bottled up, not knowing where to spill it.

But something came across that said everything was all right. I saw it in Pat's expression and in the sparkle of Velda's eyes. My buddy could read me the way old buddies can, but with Velda there was knowledge that saw other things on the inside and her eyes told me that the many past months were just that . . . past. There was no need for excuses, no need for stories to be told if I didn't want to tell them. Just that wonderful *glad you're back* look that said everything without saying anything at all.

If you didn't look closely, our greeting would have seemed perfunctory. When I shook hands with Pat, we both wanted to do it harder, but knew it wasn't time yet, and when Velda and I hugged, there was a gentle intensity we both felt. It was only a *hello* kiss to whoever saw it, but to us it was a silent explosion of flaming emotion that was almost frightening. Velda drew back modestly, and when she looked at my eyes, knew that I had felt it too.

There was a time when I would have questioned the feeling, wondering what it was. But not now. This time I knew. Very quietly, so that even Pat couldn't hear me, I said, "I love you, Velda."

And just as quickly she answered, "Yes, I know."

I waited. She smiled. Finally she said, "You *know* how I feel, don't you?" Then I waited, grinned a little bit and said, "Now I know, kitten."

2

MY APARTMENT HAD CHANGED. There was a different smell to it. The furniture was the same, but seemed brighter. The window curtains weren't the same ones I had a girl from Third Avenue put up. Velda caught me looking at them and said, "They needed changing."

I nodded as if I knew what she meant.

No dishes were in the kitchen sink and in the bathroom there was fresh soap and new towels on the rack. "I cleaned up in here," Velda said. "Then I kept it clean."

"Yes," I told her. "I could tell."

"How?" she asked me with a verbal smirk.

"The toilet seat was down," I said.

She started to laugh and when she stopped her eyes did that thing that always unnerved me somehow. It was something only a woman could do and she seemed to know just when to do it.

Her voice was low and throaty, her words soft and inviting. She let the look linger a few seconds longer, knowing what it was doing to me, then she husked, "How are you going to thank me, Mike?"

I could time a reaction, too. I knew what she wanted and what she expected me to tell her, but this was my time now and she needed something so utterly unexpected it would rock her down to her socks. It was going to rock me just as well, and for a brief second, I hoped I wasn't hopping in over my head . . . but that moment passed and the time was right now. I reached out and took both of her hands in mine. I could feel the strength and warmth and felt a little bit of a tremor too.

Very quietly I said to her, "You know what happened to me, doll. I'm all shot up and not worth a damn thing. People are going to be looking for me to make sure I'm out of it for good. Economically I'm a bad risk, though that's not a totally hopeless situation as long as I can stay alive, and believe me, that last part's not going to be easy."

Her frown was back, bewilderment clouded her eyes like she was trying to solve some strange riddle, one that had no good answer.

I took one hand away from hers, then reached up to stroke that lovely auburn hair that still rolled under at her shoulders in a soft pageboy. I said, "I want to marry you, kitten. I think I've always wanted to since you walked into my office looking for a job."

The way her hands squeezed mine told me she had had that same wanting too. Sheer surprise still showed in her eyes at having heard the totally unexpected. There was joy too, but subdued, as if she were reading my mind. "That was the good news," she said, then waited patiently for my answer.

An odd grunt came up into my throat. "We have a little longer to wait," I said.

"Why?"

"Because I have to finish something."

"Marcos Dooley?"

I nodded. "Pat tell you?"

"Everything."

"What do you want me to do, Velda?"

Without any hesitation at all, she said, "Finish it, Mike. Unless you do you won't be any good at all."

Pat had made the way easy for me. A plainclothesman I recognized met me at Bellevue Hospital and said with a grin, "You sure are like a bad penny. Everything has been nice and quiet and now you show up again."

"Maybe I can hold it down this time." I grinned back. "How's Dooley doing?"

"Dying fast, Mike. If he hadn't known you were coming in he would've been gone by now."

We got on the elevator and the cop pushed the button to our floor. "Who's got him under guard?" I asked him.

"The usual," he told me, then explained, "The DA's office has a big interest in him, but his doctor won't let them question him yet."

"The DA trying to get a fix on the Ponti bunch?"

"You got it."

"He say anything yet?"

"No. He just asked for you."

I shrugged as the car stopped and the door opened. "He knew Pat as well as he did me."

"He just asked for you, though."

"Who's on the door?"

"Nobody from the DA's squad."

When we turned the corner I saw the pair of uniforms flanking the entrance. The taller one rocked back and forth on his heels while his partner did a slow, steady survey of the corridor. They spotted us, then parted slightly to let us through. The plainclothes dick stopped at the door and motioned for me to go ahead in.

"You're not coming?" I asked him.

"He won't talk if there's anyone else around."

"The place wired?"

"No."

"How come?"

The cop let out a little laugh. "Captain Chambers and the doctor do a dance together."

"What's the tune?" I asked him.

He laughed again. "Screw the DA's office. It's a great number."

I turned the knob, went in and closed the door behind me.

The place was a death room, all right. It hung heavy in the air. Light came from the instrument panel behind the bed, the glow a pale orange yellow. You could smell the death. Not really, but you knew you could if you tried.

When my eyes adjusted to the gloom I saw the mound under the sheet and knew that was where Dooley was. Quietly, I walked over and stood beside the bed, looking down on something with a hole in it that let life leak out. His breathing was shallow but even, the pain of the gunshot being buried under the weight of narcotics.

While I was trying to figure out a way to waken him he seemed to sense he was not alone and with an effort his eyes opened, strayed vacantly a moment, then centered on me. "You made it, huh?"

"Sure, for you, Dooley. Why didn't you get Pat?"

"He's not a snake like you are."

"Come on—" I started to say, but he cut me off with a shake of his head.

"Mike . . . you're a mean slob. You're . . . nasty. You do

the damndest things anybody . . . ever heard about. Pat's not like you."

"He's a cop, Marcos."

The smile was real, but forced. "You always called me Marcos . . ."

"I know. When I was teed off at you."

"You . . . teed off at me . . . now?"

"Pal, after taking those slugs myself, I haven't got enough left to get sore at anything. Right now I'm a pussycat."

"But you're sort of thinking . . . why I had to see you."

"Sort of."

"Uh-huh." He coughed lightly and his face twitched with pain. My eyes were almost fully adjusted to the gloom now and could see him clearly. The years hadn't been good to him at all and the final indignity of getting shot had drained him completely.

A full minute passed before the pain was gone, but now there was a clock ticking behind his eyes. I knew it and he knew it. Each tick took him closer to the end. He strained to see me again, finally found my eyes. "Mike . . . remember Don Angelo?"

I thought he was drifting back along memory lane. Don Angelo had been dead for twenty years. At the age of ninety-some he had died in peace in his Brooklyn apartment, surrounded by his real family. His *other* family was a hundredfold larger, spread out over the East Coast domain the don called his own.

"Sure, Dooley. What about him?"

His expression looked strained and there was shame in his eyes. There was a long pause before he said, "I worked for him, Mike."

It was hard to believe. "You, Dooley?"

"I wasn't lucky . . . like you and Pat. Don Angelo . . .

found out . . . about me being in Army Intelligence. He had work for me."

"Dooley," I asked him, "what kind of work would you do for the mob? You were no gunhand. You never messed around in illegal business."

He held his hand up again and I stopped talking. "It was . . . a different . . . kind of business." My silent nod asked him a question and he answered it. "Do you know . . . what the yearly take . . . of the . . ." He groped for the words and said, "associated mobs . . . adds up to?"

"Internal Revenue Service collects statistics like that."

"And . . . ?"

"It's a pile of loot," I said.

"Mike," he said very solemnly, "you haven't got the slightest idea."

"What are you getting at, Dooley?"

His chest rose under the sheet while he took several deep breaths, his eyes closing until whatever spasm it was had calmed down. When he looked up his mouth worked a bit before the words came out.

"It was back before all the trouble, Mike. Remember when the young guys tried to take over . . . the family business?"

"But they didn't make it, Dooley."

"No . . . not then." He sucked in another big lungful of air. "But it made the dons think."

"Yeah," I reminded him, "they were all going legitimate then. The business went *Big Business*."

Somehow, the smile he gave me made me feel pretty ignorant. He let me stew in it for a few seconds and I hoped he was enjoying his moment because I surely wasn't.

"The original five families met in Miami. They . . . had researched the situation . . . checked out the books with independent counsel as the government likes to say."

"What are you getting to, Dooley?"

Once again, he gave out a grunt, this time of satisfaction. "They . . . were all getting screwed . . . by their kids. The ones they put through college. The ones they . . . tapped to run the businesses . . . when they handed it over."

"The dons weren't *that* dumb," I interrupted.

"Computers," Dooley said.

"Computers!"

"They learned . . . how to use them . . . in college. They didn't want to wait. They wanted it *now* . . . and were getting it. Now shut up and don't talk until I'm finished."

"And the chronicle continues," I muttered.

"You had to get that in," he told me.

"I don't like it when somebody tells me to shut up," I said with mock indignity. Then added, "But now I'm shut up."

"Okay. Stay that way . . . and listen. All the old dons . . . never exploited their wealth. They might spend it, but they never looked like . . . they had a dime. Lousy little apartments, their wives did the cleaning and cooking. If they had big times it was when . . . they went back to . . . the old country. The kids . . . the bad ones . . . knew they had it, but they didn't know where the dons kept it." He was starting to breathe with an unnatural rhythm and I didn't like it, but there was no way to stop him now. "That was when . . . they got hold of me." He knew what I wanted to ask, but shook his head again. "Later . . . you'll find out why. It isn't . . . important now."

A little red light flashed on the panel behind his head. It stayed on about two seconds then went off. Nobody came in so I ignored it.

He said, "Nobody really knows . . . how they did it. Cash and valuables got moved by truck with different crews so that no one knew where it came from or where it was going. Except the last crew."

"What happened to them?"

"Like the old pirate days. Their skeletons are still there. When their job . . . was done . . . so were they." He rolled his eyes up to mine again. "Now stay shut up . . . okay?"

I gave him the nod again. "All their heavy money . . . was in paper. They cashed in everything they had and turned it into dollars. They pulled out . . . all their numbered accounts in Switzerland, Bahamas, Cayman. The cash flow was still coming in from gambling and drugs and all that . . . crap, you know?" I nodded again. "That's what fooled . . . the young bucks. The . . . walking around money was there, but the capital had disappeared."

"Can I talk now?" I asked him.

"Go ahead." He seemed a little breathless and glad for the break.

"When did they find out?"

"Maybe six months before the shootup you were in. The computers came up with it. At first they . . . they thought it was . . . like a mistake. When the machines said no way, then they . . . thought they were being ripped off. The stuff . . . really hit the fan then. All those hot shots liked to go nuts. Now . . . let's see what you remember."

All I could do was watch and wait. But he made sense. There was a genuine unrest in the upper echelons of the underworld fraternity a couple years ago. Everything was cloaked in total secrecy that even had the IRS concerned. No matter how hard they dug into mob records they kept coming up blank.

Dooley said, "The dons were getting old by then. When they . . . died off it all . . . seemed natural. Their deaths were the things old men were supposed to die of. You know, strokes, heart attacks, falls down stairs."

"I remember that. There was a regular parade of those gaudy funerals for a while."

And it was a time to remember. Every newspaper and television station covered the rows of flower-laded Cadillacs and the rivers of tears the bereaved shed at the gravesites. The families all kept long faces, not letting a smile show through, but inwardly, with each successive carnival, the happy light in their eyes began to show and they all waited to see who the new king would be.

While I was thinking these thoughts I was looking straight down at Dooley and he read my thoughts perfectly.

"I was . . . working for Lorenzo Ponti by then, Mike. Ponti was the . . . smart one. He was in charge of . . . the big operation. He moved faster than the young kids . . . he kept ahead of everybody, that guy."

"Did he move right in when the others died?" I asked him.

"Hell, Mike, they didn't . . . just die. They were killed. All of them. Except Ponti. And when *he* goes there won't be any more dons . . . just the young phonies who are going to be howling mad because their inheritance has disappeared. Poof! Just . . . like that." He tried to snap his fingers, but didn't have the strength.

"Dooley . . . doesn't Lorenzo Ponti know where this hoard is?"

"He thinks he does."

"But somebody faked him out?"

"Me," Dooley told me. "I faked . . . him out. I changed the road signs . . . covered up paths, disguised everything. Someday you'll find out. Ponti will be digging in the wrong mountain."

Suddenly sheer, raw pain flashed across his face and his back arched under the cover. He was beginning to look down his own black alley now and it was too fearful to believe.

"Mike . . . these doctors . . ."

He seemed to choke on his voice and closed his eyes. When he forced them open there was a deep seriousness to his gaze. I said, "They're good men, Dooley. The best."

"But I'm not a good guy."

"They don't care. You're here and you're their patient."

"Why won't they tell me anything?"

"Maybe they haven't finished their tests yet."

"Baloney, Mike. They gave me something in the IV and I can't feel anything anymore." Now his eyes had an anguished look. "You know where I got . . . shot, don't you?"

"Pat told me," I said.

"Don't lie to me . . . how bad . . . is it?"

"Bad," I told him. There was no sense holding back. He could see it in my face.

"Tell me."

"Three hollow point slugs took you down."

"Tore me apart, didn't it?"

Once again, all I could do was nod.

"Why didn't they tell me that?"

"Because they're doctors. They have hope."

"They're not here . . . now."

"You're supposed to be resting."

"Come off it, Mike. I'm supposed to be . . . dying. I can feel it coming on, so don't give me any crap. I got no insides left anymore. My guts are gone, right?"

"Right," I said.

"How much time, Mike." It wasn't a question. He wasn't asking for words of hope or consolation. He had some bigger purpose in mind.

I said, "Any minute, kiddo. You're close. They probably think it's better if you just drifted off alone. It won't hurt."

His smile was brief and there was a small glow of relief on his face. "Listen to me," he said. "What would you do . . . if you had . . . eighty-nine *billion* dollars?"

"Buy a new car," I told him.

"I said . . . eighty-nine *billion,* Mike."

Facetious words that started to come out stopped at my lips. His eyes were clear now and stared hard into mine. There was that strange expression on his face too. And he was dying. There was no doubt about that at all. What he said now wouldn't be a lie.

Softly, I said, "Only a government has that kind of money, Dooley."

He didn't argue about it. "That's right," he agreed. "It's a government, all right. It's got people and taxes and soldiers and more money than anyone . . . can imagine. But nobody sees it and they . . . don't want to be seen."

When I scowled at him he knew I had gotten the message. Only his eyes smiled back until the pain started showing. It was the diluted agony of a medicated death. He didn't want me to speak because he had more to say and no time to say it in. "They left eighty-nine *billion,* Mike. *Billion,* you know? I know where it is. *They* don't." Before I could speak I saw the spark begin to go out.

His voice was suddenly soft. It had the muted quality of great importance and I leaned forward to hear him better. He said, "You can . . . find out . . . where it is." His eyes never closed. They just quietly got dead.

Pat was waiting for me in the lobby. I didn't have to tell him Dooley was gone. It was written all over my face. The half-healed wounds in my side had a new ache to them, the flesh being drawn tight from the tension of watching while an old buddy died. When I thought of what he had told me a creeping river of pain seemed to flow from my body to my brain and I stopped, holding on to the back of a chair.

Pat said, "You all right?"

"No problems," I lied. "Too much walking."

"Baloney. Sit down."

I took a seat beside him and forced some controlled breaths. A couple of minutes later I felt myself going back to normal.

Pat knew when it happened. "Was it bad?"

I nodded. "He was hurting. Damn, he was *really* hurting." I turned my head and looked at him hard. "How'd he get it, Pat?"

"How come you never asked before?"

"I didn't know if I could take it or not. I had just been down that road myself."

"Now you're okay?"

"I'm fine, Pat."

"Okay. He was home alone. He had come in from a solo supper a little after nine o'clock, apparently read the paper and made out four monthly bills. He was on his fifth and last when he died. There were no powder burns on his body, so it wasn't a close-up shot. The impacts knocked him right out of his chair. When he went down he took the phone with him accidentally. The receiver was off the hook, but the base was right beside his hand and he dialed 911 and managed to tell the operator he was shot. They traced the call and got him to the hospital. He was unconscious until a few hours before you got here. The doctors didn't want him to have *any* visitors."

"He recognize who shot him?"

"Apparently not. It was an easy hit, though. The door was unlocked. Someone just gave it a shove, opened it enough to see Dooley sitting there about fifteen feet away and pumped three slugs into him from a .357. The perp had plenty of time to get away clean and so far no witnesses have come forward with any information."

"Any trace on the slugs?"

"No. Just about any gun shop carries them."

"What did the lab technicians come up with?"

"Nothing. The shooter never set foot in the room. There was powder residue on the door jamb and the edge of the door itself, so it was pretty apparent how it was done."

"What's your opinion, Pat?"

His eyes drooped a moment in thought, then: "Considering the background, somebody was very lucky. He tell you who he worked for?"

"Yeah," I said, "he told me. Lorenzo Ponti was his boss, but his work wasn't inside the mob. He was—"

"I know," Pat cut in. "He was a field hand, a handyman on Ponti's estate. We checked out his social security records first thing and it was all down there. He tell you that?"

"That's right." I didn't add to it. Not yet, anyway. Dooley's last words were meant for me alone. If he had wanted us both to know he would have said so.

"But he said more, didn't he?" Pat stated deliberately.

Again, I nodded. "He told me there was trouble in the ranks."

"There's always trouble there."

"Not like this. The trouble is fraternal, as if the kids were ganging up on the parents."

"We know about that. Something's been brewing for the last six years. There are still guys running the organization who have their feet in the wrong century. Now the younger ones want their share of the power."

"Think they'll get it, Pat?"

"Eventually. If they can't force the issue they'll finally inherit it."

"How many of the old dons are dead or in retirement?"

"You read the papers, Mike. Not more than a handful are around. Some of them went down in odd ways, but old age can do that to a person. Besides, who cared if they kicked off or not?"

Pat let out a grunt and stretched his legs. "What have you got on your mind, Mike?"

"There was a motive for Dooley's death, pal."

Pat's nod was very solemn. "He was into a bookie for fifty-five hundred bucks."

"Who?"

"Marty Diamond."

"Nuts, Marty isn't like that and you know it."

"Word had it he used some loan sharks a couple of times."

"A lot of people do. Nobody messed up Dooley so he probably paid off his debts."

"He was murdered, Mike," Pat reminded me, "so there was a motive. It could have been something he heard or something he saw, but it cost him his life."

I wanted to tell Pat it could have been something he *did*, but I didn't want to dig any holes in the playing field. Not yet, anyway. "So what's your opinion?" I asked him.

"Well, you knew him as much as I did. He was an okay guy, but he lived with some strange company. Outside of being one hell of a soldier, he had no special talents. He never had command duties, but he was great in the field on special assignments. Now where does that get you in civilian life?"

"How much did he make working for Ponti?"

Pat screwed his face up and looked at me. "That was a big surprise. He made more than I do, but I can see why.

We had a look at Ponti's work sheets and Dooley really kept his estates in order. He could hire guys to help him if he needed to, any supplies he needed he could order directly, his time was his own, and nobody ever complained about his work."

"I guess he was cut out for more than we thought," I said. "What did he do in New York?"

"Not much. Work was out on Long Island or upstate on the apple farm. Ponti had a couple of places in Jersey, but sold them some years ago. Ponti is one old don who likes his Sicilian feet down deep in the earth." He paused, leaned back and gazed at the ceiling for a couple of seconds, then said, "What are you holding back, Mike?"

"What makes you think that?"

"Because you're the only guy I know who always wears crepe rubber soles on his shoes. Nobody ever hears you walking. The original gumshoe, always sneaking up on somebody."

"Not on you, pal."

"Come on, you've been on top of some pretty big cases and I've always wondered how the hell you did it. You've gotten ahead of the local cops, the feds and a few other agencies—"

"Not all the time," I interrupted.

"Enough to make me think about it."

"I try not to get side-tracked, Pat. I only take one problem at a time."

"Yeah, I know. You chew it to pieces until you can swallow it." He gave me that stare again. "Then you shoot somebody," he added.

I knew he was going to say that. He was right, too. And so far so was I. The courts had picked me apart and the press had a field day with me, but that was before I had my guts churned up by .357 slugs. *The same kind that killed*

Dooley. But that was pure coincidence at this point. Magnum-style pistols were all over the streets these days and no matter how many laws were passed they were going to stay available to anybody who had the money for them.

"I'm not doing any more shooting, Pat. I can't even carry a piece on that side anymore."

He was going to say something, but stopped and gave me an odd, sideways look. It wasn't what I said, but the way I said it. Finally, he accepted it and got to his feet. But it wasn't an acceptance that lasted very long. He let out a laugh and ran his fingers through his hair. "Man, what a con artist you are," he told me.

I grinned at him and got up myself.

"What're you doing tomorrow, Mike?"

"I'll be at the office. Why?"

"Maybe I'll stop by. We need to do some talking. Sometimes I get to be like you and have one of those feelings that give me a chill."

"Not you, Pat," I said sarcastically.

"Yeah, me, and this is one of them. This time a dead man doesn't put you against the world all by yourself. I'm involved in this too. It's an open NYPD homicide, but there are some angles to it that put a color on it that isn't in the spectrum."

"Like what?" I demanded softly.

"Like you, pal," he said, "like you. If I didn't know you were still one of the walking wounded we'd be talking downtown, but you're getting a break. I'll see you tomorrow in your office. Now get your tail home and try sleeping. You're going to need it. And tell Velda to cool it."

An odd excitement was building in me as I walked toward my office door. The entire floor had been refurbished, pastel-painted and softened with a thick carpet.

Nothing had chunks taken out of it and all the glass in the area was whole. My lease still had another year to run, but it wasn't the kind of place I'd pick for the work I was in. The excitement wasn't about the office at all. It was because Velda would be there.

I pushed open the door and there she was behind her desk, chin propped in her hands, watching me. I said, "Am I supposed to say good afternoon or kiss you?"

"You can do whatever you like." I got that impish grin again.

"No, I can't."

"Why not?"

"I'd get arrested," I told her.

She gave me an insolent moue and pointed at my private quarters. "The arresting officer is in there."

But I went over and kissed the top of her head before I went in. Pat Chambers was comfortably folded into my nice big office chair, his feet up on a half-opened desk drawer, drinking one of my cold Miller Lite beers like he owned the place.

"I hope that wasn't the last one, Pat."

"Velda slipped in two fresh six-packs. Some doll you got there, pal. Congratulations."

"She told you?"

"Are you kidding?" Pat said. "All you have to do is look at her face." He paused and shook his head. "Trouble is, the way she's built it's hard to get to her face." He took another pull from the can and nodded at the small refrigerator. "Going to join me?"

"You might have found me," I said, "but you didn't pull my medical records. All that good stuff is just for looking at right now."

"Why have you got it on ice?"

"It's for the clients," I told him.

"Oh. You going to tell me how you did with Dooley?"

I pulled a chair away from the wall and sat down. "He practically died in my arms, Pat. Didn't he have anybody else?"

"You know Dooley. He always was a loner. I wondered why he didn't call for me."

I let a few seconds pass, then: "You *really* want to know?"

He set the beer down on my blotter and squinted at me. "Sure I do!" he said. "Hell, after all we went through together you'd think—"

"Pat . . . Dooley thought you were too soft."

"For what?"

"To do what has to be done," I said.

I sat there and studied my friend. Pat Chambers, a captain in the homicide division. Still young, but almost of retirement age. Smart, streetwise, college educated, superbly trained in the nuances of detection. Tough, but not *killing tough.* His conscience was still finely honed and that's what Dooley had meant. There was no way now that I could tell him what Dooley had told me.

Pat picked up the beer can and emptied it in two swallows. There was nothing else in the wastebasket under the desk so it made a clanking sound when it hit bottom. "He wanted you to nail the guy who shot him," he said flatly.

"Something like that," I replied.

"There's a lot of street talk over who wiped out Azi Ponti, Mike. A witness saw you get shot, but you jerked back from the initial impact and caved in at the second. The witness never actually saw who killed Azi Ponti, so it could be assumed a random shot got him."

"The bullet that killed him was never recovered?"

"Azi had no top of his head left and in that area there was little chance of recovering anything. It could have gone into the river or lodged in a building somewhere. Who knows?"

"I know," I said.

"You know what?"

"I shot the punk. I took him out with one fat cap and ball .45."

"That's what I figured," Pat told me, "but if I were you, I'd keep it to myself. Now tell me this . . . why were you there at all?"

I ran through all the details I had given Dr. Morgan when I had recovered enough to discuss the situation. Pat wanted to know about the snitch who had put me onto the Gaetano-Ponti rumble, but the old guy wasn't important at all. He just happened to be in the right place to overhear something that wasn't supposed to be overheard. He got shook up and passed it on to me.

Pat digested all that I told him then turned and stared at me. "It doesn't matter, Mike. Both Ugo and his old man have picked you out as the shooter."

"They picked well," I said.

"They're pretty damn potent enemies, buddy."

"Nobody better," I said.

"The old man can pull strings and call the shots, but Ugo is the bad one. In the time you've been out of it that punk has gone plain crazy."

I was thinking of what Dooley had told me. "I can understand it," I said.

Pat didn't quite get my meaning on that. He said, "You know what they call him, don't you?"

"No," I answered quizzically, "what?"

"Bulletproof Ponti."

"Who calls him that, for Pete's sake? I never heard that on the streets."

Pat let out a short laugh. "It doesn't come off the

streets. It's *our* guys who call him that. Twice we had shoot-outs with a perp identified as Ugo Ponti and the officers said they had direct hits on him but he didn't go down."

"Were these *positive* IDs?" I asked him.

"No. It was night, close to twelve both times, but the visibility was good."

"What was going on, Pat?"

"All we can figure was a drug connection. We think Ugo was there to intercept somebody who wasn't paying off and Ugo was the enforcer. His luck was lousy. Both times he was spotted by passing prowl cars who slowed up to investigate and got fired on. The officers returned the fire from the protection of their vehicles, saw the target stagger, then back off into the shadows. When they converged on the area he was gone. No blood spots, no evidence, nothing."

"What were they shooting with?"

"The new weaponry. Heavy stuff."

"Regulation ammo?"

"They said so, but nobody pressed the issue. I wouldn't blame them for using hot loads, though."

I leaned back in the chair and stared across the desk. I was about to ask the question, but Pat saw it coming and beat me to it. "We found all the slugs that were fired in one action."

"All?"

"Every one. Some had smashed against the brick wall, three went into the woodwork and a couple into a metal garbage can."

I waited, then, finally, he said it. "Two didn't have the expected contours."

"Oh?" This time he waited until I asked, "Cloth marks?"

"Possibly."

"You think he was wearing body armor?"

He cocked his head and shrugged. "If it was Ugo, he would have known we don't use the old .38's anymore. The new stuff will penetrate ordinary armor."

"Even what the SWAT teams wear?"

"That depends on a lot of factors. Distance, caliber . . . you know what I mean?"

"But if he *did* have on body armor, it sure worked. Ugo Ponti is still around and not showing any wear and tear."

Pat nodded. "Explain that."

"Don't you have anything in your ballistics library on it?"

"I checked."

"So?"

Pat said, "One of the U.S. firms came up with a new technology. It was a vast improvement, but it wasn't merchandised properly, or our buyers had their heads up their tails. I think it was the British that bought into it."

"What was different about it?"

"For one thing, it was about four times as effective in stopping a bullet. The bulk . . . the size factor . . . was minimal and the weight was negligible. Nobody would know you were wearing it, and as long as you didn't get hit in the head, you were safe. The bad part was the price. I understand it was considerable, out of the range of ordinary people. On top of that the technology is very restrictive. Super secret. They probably keep it for the royals or extremely high-risk projects."

"Let's not call the bad guys ordinary people, Pat," I told him. "One thing they have is a lot of that 'considerable' stuff, and that can buy a lot of secrets. Have you pulled Ugo in since then?"

"It took a month to find him after the supposed first time. He was down in Mexico on a vacation. The second time he came home after six weeks from a junket in Canada."

"No passports needed, right?"

"Right. Just a visa for Mexico. We know the old man was pretty well pissed off at him, but he's the apple of his eye and there was no rough stuff. The kid even let us give him a physical, but there were no injury marks on him. Clever, huh?"

"Yeah." I stood up and stretched. "His alibis good?"

"Of course. Ponti has good liars on his side."

"What's the official version on all this? The DA's office ought to be saying something."

"They sure ought to, but they're not. In that ruckus on the waterfront the dead and the shooters became one big package. They cancelled each other out. It was blamed as a gang war and none of the dead are going to be missed."

"Not even me?"

Pat said, "Strangely enough, you didn't draw bad press. The papers publicized your history and since they couldn't figure out what you were doing there, they played you down." He swung his feet off the desk drawer and planted them on the floor. "Some of the reporters knew about that beef you had with Lorenzo Ponti."

"Hell, Pat, that wasn't a beef. It was a job. I had to find out who really owned those four buildings on Fifth Avenue. So it was old Lorenzo. Big deal. There were no back taxes to be paid or shady dealings in the purchase. Those threats came because he thought I was prying in his personal affairs."

"You didn't have to manhandle him in his own nightclub, for Pete's sake!"

"He didn't have to give me any lip, either."

"Come on, Mike, he had his own gunnies there."

"Yeah, but I had him, my back was against the wall and I had my own rod where I could get it."

"You were lucky, kiddo."

"The heck I was. I had Ponti in front of me. He would have been the first one hit."

"Then you would have bought it."

I let my teeth show through my grin. "Pat . . . you keep forgetting something."

"Like what?"

"Like that reputation I have. I'm a real big shooter, Pat. I have all the clippings to prove it."

"You have scars too."

"But I'm still here, pal."

"For how long?"

"We'll worry about that when the chips go down," I said.

3

THERE WAS NO WAY I could have escaped the coming-out party. New York was still a tabloid town, even with the *Times* running the show. The subway crowd still wanted their photos and the combination of local and network TV newscasters fought for camera space if anything had an offbeat flavor to it.

And I sure was offbeat.

Velda called the DA's office first and told them to shove their demands to have me go to their office. I was still "in recovery" and they either came to my office or forget it. They made the appointment for ten and it was nine-thirty now.

In a way, I had a little celebrity status hanging on from the old days, but not enough to jolt the head man into doing any interrogating . . . unless he knew he could slap an arrest warrant on me and make it stick. To him, I was interesting, but old news and the election wasn't until next year anyway.

Had he known Velda or the hungry reporters he would have been on the spot soaking up the news coverage, but, like always, politicians weren't that smart unless bands were playing and flags were flying in their faces. My office was packed with TV teams, cameras set up, lighting arranged, and half had already gotten information down for voice-over commentary on the early broadcasts. Most of that would be running with the post-action shots of the riverfront rumble.

Exactly at ten the squad from the DA's office arrived, four of them walking two abreast. They walked in formation, but they weren't in step, and all I could think of was why government lawyers have to look like a toy mechanical rabbit advertising batteries on TV. They could have carried signs, at least.

Florence Lake led the pack. Her suit matched the others except for the skirt and she didn't seem too happy about being different. When she saw the mob scene in the office the outrage hit her face with a deep flush and the cords in her neck showed as they pulled her face into a wooden mask. The others were junior executive types and didn't seem to mind at all. Any coverage was good publicity for them.

The TV teams and reporters had already been alerted and were damn well aware of the confrontation. They were going to enjoy this, especially if somebody could stick a needle in the DA lady's behind.

Florence Lake knew the angles too. She was all smiles and politeness and asked for a few minutes alone with me inside my private quarters and seemed very pleased when everybody was glad to agree. Pleased? She was burning up.

I glanced over at Velda. She was holding back a grin and gave me the knife-across-the-throat gesture to lay on the Lake broad during the interview. And that was easy to do. I gave her a lot of color and nothing she didn't already know. But she *was* a lawyer and she was smart enough to know that there was something more to be had, but she didn't know where to probe.

Florence Lake didn't take notes. Her assistant did that. She gave me an intimidating look and said, "Your reason for being there doesn't seem quite valid, Mr. Hammer."

"Look," I told her, "you know how it is when you get a tip. You want to check it out first to make sure it hasn't got a spin on it."

"Your informant wasn't reliable?"

"He could tell you where the nearest bar was, or how to scrounge up enough for a drink on a rainy day. It was a tip given offhand and I wasn't concerned with reliability."

"Then what *did* concern you?"

"Having those hard cases think I might have set Lorenzo Ponti up for a hit."

"Your altercation with him was that serious?"

"Only to his ego, ma'am. It wasn't physical and it didn't cost him any money, but some of these old-country types have a lot of misplaced pride and you don't want to mess with that."

"So you only went to the waterfront to warn him?"

"Yes."

Her expression said she didn't believe me at all. "What made you think Mr. Ponti would take your word for it?"

"He wasn't dumb, ma'am."

She changed the subject abruptly. "Who shot you?"

I wasn't under oath, so I could tell her anything I wanted. I did it in a noncommittal way with a shrug of my shoulders. I said, "It was dark. The area is hardly lit, as you know."

"Yes." There was another pause. "Did you fire your gun?"

"Why do you assume I had a gun?"

"Because you are licensed to carry one."

"A lot of private investigators don't carry them."

"But you're Mike Hammer," she said lightly

When I let a grin crease my mouth she didn't like it a bit. "True," I said. "But I got shot right in the beginning of that mess. Two hits in soft, deadly places."

Florence Lake was looking at me as if I were the biggest liar in the world and she was about to expose me to the world. Before she could, I pulled the shirt out of my pants and lifted it up, my fingers going under the bandage I had lightly taped down, and when I leaned back in my chair she got a good look at the scarred, ugly mess on my belly that was still runny with a pinkish discharge and dotted with tiny stitch marks that held it all together. Right now, it needed a lot of taking care of, but it looked worse than it was, disgusting enough to make the lady DA's face contort with a spasm as her guts churned and she damn near vomited on her own feet. It didn't bother the other three. They all leaned forward in curiosity, like they were appreciating some artwork.

I put my shirt back and I thought she was going to thank me.

She had only lost her composure momentarily. As if nothing happened, she asked, "Who took care of that wound?"

Again, the shrug. "I didn't gain consciousness for over a week."

"You knew where you were?"

"Uh-huh. In a medical facility somewhere. I really didn't care."

"Who attended you?"

"I knew it was a male. He wasn't young, at least that was my impression."

"You do have a bill for services."

"No. I will probably get one. I said probably. Somebody could have taken care of me out of the goodness of his heart."

"And *probably* not," she said, then added, "At least none that I know."

"What difference does it make?"

"He could be a witness to a murder."

"Whose?"

"The man who shot you."

"Lady, I don't know who that was." I lied, but there was no way she could prove it. "Besides, I don't have the slugs that got me."

"The doctor should. A legitimate doctor wouldn't destroy evidence like that."

I didn't back off. "He could have been a vet, ma'am, or a medical student. Or maybe some old retired guy who decided to keep his hand in but was a little shook up about what had happened." At least I was closer to the truth there. "I already told you, I was out of it. I was moved down to Florida into something like a rental beach house. Most of the time I was sedated. I was alone for a long while, just healing up."

"What made you come back?"

Another white lie. "I read *The Daily News* somebody had dropped near the house. A good friend of mine had been murdered. We had been in the army together and I wanted to go to the funeral."

"Who was the person?" she asked me.

"Marcos Dooley." Her assistant wrote the name down. Later he would check it out.

For half a minute it was quiet. Nobody spoke and she

never took her eyes off me. She retracted the tip of the ballpoint pen she kept in her fingers for effect, then said, "You know, of course, we could take you downtown and hammer all this out in great detail."

I nodded. "Sure, I know that, but I wouldn't tell you anything more or different. Besides . . ." and I gave her a big grin again, "with all those cameras doing the local color out there and ready to catch all the action they can get, I don't think it would be a good idea, do you?"

She forced a smile and stood up. The rest of the coterie was on its feet immediately. "I didn't know this was going to be a press conference, Mr. Hammer," she said. "The next time we'll make it more private."

You didn't have to spell it out for the newssharks. They got the picture right away. When the door opened the buzz of conversation died down and the little tight-lipped smiles began. A couple of floodlights went on and their cameras turned, but it was for file copy only unless something really big came out of my return.

When I went out there it wasn't like that at all and we had a swinging press conference. I told them nothing different or new, but laid it on the way an audience would enjoy it. They got twelve minutes on tape before I ran out of steam and my belly started to hurt again. It showed in my face and they closed the show down with big smiles.

It was great to be back.

I showered unhurriedly, letting the hot water from the needle spray massage fresh life back into me. When I dried off I climbed into fresh underwear and opened the closet door to a rack of suits cleaned and pressed, shoes shined and laid out on the floor rack, shirts and ties in the right places and a new trench coat with a wintery lining still zipped in. All I could think of was that my secretary really knew how to take care of a guy. Then, for a few seconds I just froze, wondering if I could stand all that attention, then thought, what the heck, we both have to give in a little.

Velda never knew where I kept my guns in a built-in hidden compartment inside the closet and they were just as I had left them. The Gold Cup .45 and the Colt Combat Commander lay wrapped side by side, four full clips of ammo ready to go. All the accessories were waiting, but it wasn't gun time anymore. That hurting place in my gut told me that. I picked up a loaded clip with chrome-cast .45s and slipped it into my pocket. It wasn't much, but I felt a little more normal with some weight on that side.

But who was I kidding? Carrying slugs without a gun was like wearing a yachting hat without having a boat. Ah, hell, I thought, I felt better so I did it anyway.

Outside, it was cool enough for the trench coat, but without the lining. Florida had gotten me spoiled. For a few minutes I stood in front of the building and watched the traffic go by. It was only six-thirty and the traffic flow seemed normal. I turned right, walking toward the corner where the angled window of a dress shop did a mirror reflection of what was behind me.

Nobody was there at all. I flagged down a cab and gave Velda's address.

A half hour before I had taken the pill dosage on Frank Morgan's list. The day had been hectic enough that I felt like I could use the two little pink ones he suggested for the purpose. The only trouble was, he didn't tell me to stay home afterward. Whatever those little buggers were, they were giving me a funny feeling. I called Velda from the lobby of her building and she came down within two minutes, a big, luscious woman who could turn any man's head and give every woman a touch of envy. She didn't have that touch of youthful naïveté any longer. She wore sheer full-bloomed womanhood like a cape, her eyes that same deep brown, reflecting an intelligence that was beautifully female.

We didn't kiss. She simply hooked her arm under mine and gave me a squeeze that said a lot of things, a muscular, sensual gesture that made me go all shaky. "Cut that out," I said softly.

"I didn't do anything," she answered.

"The heck you didn't."

Her smile had a provocative touch to it. "Boy," she told me, "are *you* going to be easy to please."

There's no answering a newly engaged woman who's filled with gut-churning love. A man can't seem to respond to that kind of emotion, so I just opened the door to the cab that drove up to the canopy, helped her in and told the cabbie to take us to Le Cirque.

Velda moved closer to me and said, "We're going fancy tonight, aren't we?"

"Don't get too used to it, kitten."

In ten minutes we were on Sixty-fifth Street and joined the early dinner crowd edging up to the door. Out of habit I took one last look around before we went in, just in time to see two men stepping out of a black limousine, one on each side, speaking to others who hadn't emerged yet. Both guys were in their early forties, well dressed and styled with class. They were loaded with money and welcome at any place in town, but these two bums worked the legitimate side of Lorenzo Ponti's business in Manhattan. They had come over the line from the old muscle days when they were young hoods and into an area well protected by professional business personnel and all the legal machinery that money could buy. One was Howie

Drago and the other one was Leonard Patterson. But they were still punks.

The captain was an old friend and held out his hand to me. His first look at Velda almost floored him, but his attitude was very appreciative and he gave me one of those *how do you do it* looks and I just winked at him. We got a table upstairs, picking one in a far corner. The early evening news would have splashed me all over the tube again, but Le Cirque's customers saw enough people on TV sitting next to them and wouldn't make a big thing of it.

Then while the waiter was taking our drink orders I saw Velda frown, her eyes catching something behind my back. I didn't look. I waited until she said, "Patterson and Drago just came in. They're three tables over."

"I wonder if the company is coincidental or deliberate."

"Think they come in here often?" Velda queried.

"Maybe," I told her, "I could ask."

"Who did you tell about us coming here, Mike?"

"Nobody. I called and got a reservation, that's all."

The drinks came, we toasted each other silently, tasted the iced tea and stared at each other, thinking the same thing. As we looked down at the menu she said, "The office phone could have been tapped. Someone in the TV bunch could be doing a big favor."

"It's nice to be wanted," I said. "Somebody is working fast. They're quicker than the IRS."

Supper was served and I enjoyed my homecoming meal like turkey on a major holiday. Florida may have a lot of sun and some great seafood restaurants, but this was real New York eating at its best. We went through dessert and were working on the coffee when Velda said, "Can you hear them, Mike?"

"Who?"

"The group who came in the limo."

There was a quiet hum of conversation going on in the room. The early crowd never was very boisterous so I didn't have to listen hard to pick them out. It had to be deliberate. Not loud enough to be told to keep it down, but just enough so I would overhear what was being said. My name was clear enough. The nastiness that went with it was even clearer.

I said, "They drinking?"

"Martinis. They've been hard at it since they got here."

"How are the girls taking it?"

"They look a little nervous."

"I imagine so," I said.

She reached out and put her hand on top of mine. "Mike . . . what are you going to do?"

"Nothing."

She was scared now. "Mike, stop it. You never do *nothing*."

But I couldn't stop it. I was pushing back my chair and was on my feet before she could say anything else. I took it nice and easy walking across the room to that table and I knew they were watching every step I took. Howie's face was plain to read. I was just a washed-up PI with a hole in his gut and not enough left to tangle with someone a lot younger. Leonard Patterson was the big mouth and he wore a silent sneer because I had lost a lot of weight and was drained out from the medical treatment.

This had to be a good one. Velda was watching and the hard boys were ready to move. Their two women sat stiff and still, but the panic showed in their immobility. It wasn't supposed to be like this at all. When I stood over Patterson I saw his expression get a little wary and knew I had him. He had heard too many stories about me. He had read too many newspapers and what was happening right now was putting everything right on the edge.

I didn't say a word. I slid my hand into my jacket pocket and let them see the clip, then flipped out a chrome-cased .45, turned it in my fingers and set it down on its primer base beside his hand. I looked at Howie, then at Patterson, grinned so they could see the edges of my teeth then walked back to my table.

When I sat down I waved for my check. At the other table the foursome was already getting ready to go. The women seemed furious. The men weren't looking our way at all. They went out without looking back.

The waiter came with my check and I laid a nice tip on him and picked it up. We detoured past their empty table on the way out. Velda asked, "What did you say to them?"

"Nothing," I told her. The .45 slug was still there where I left it. I picked it up and dropped it back into my pocket. "I didn't have to say a thing."

She knew what had happened then. All she said to me was, "Damn!"

I had the driver wait while I walked Velda to the apartment. When I gave her a light good night kiss her eyes were asking for more. But I said, "It isn't going to be easy getting through this engagement, kitten, but let's keep it cool until we do."

"I hope you're saying that because you're still weak."

I gave her another grin, flipped out Patterson's .45 and pressed it into her palm. "Sure I am, doll, sure I am," I said.

She looked at the slug, smiled and dropped it in her cleavage where it fell into her bra. I suppose.

By the time I got home I knew it was a lie. The day had washed me out and even pushing the button in the elevator was hard work. The pain in my belly was coming back, sharp jabs of it with each beat of my pulse. When I got inside I started the bathwater going, then got undressed so there would be no waiting period before I got covered by the soothing warmth of the suds.

I should have listened to Morgan. My body wasn't fifteen years old anymore. It was injured and hurting bad and all I could do was sweat it out until nature fused with medication and I could reach a normal peak again. Twice, I had to run more hot water into the tub and an hour later the relief started. I sat there for another ten minutes, then eased out and sat under the infrared light in the ceiling until I was dried off.

Even thinking about what could have happened at Le Cirque gave me the jumps. Either of those guys could have cleaned my plow if they had gotten past my reputation. Luckily, all they could see was that single .45 slug. If I had a bullet, then I had a gun. If I had a gun, then I sure would have used it if those clowns had made a move. That was real positive thinking for them. For me it was stupid. I looked at my face in the mirror over the sink. It was pretty haggard looking. I said, "No more, Mikey boy. Quit being a wise guy."

4

VELDA WAS ALREADY AT THE OFFICE when Pat and I walked in. It was ten after nine, a breakfast of coffee and hard rolls was ready for us, then we would see Marcos Dooley off at the funeral parlor. I asked Pat about the flowers and he said, "Dooley left orders. No flowers. He said it reminded him of a funeral."

"Since when did he think ahead, Pat?"

"He'd changed in the last few years. I found out from the director at Richmond's that he had paid for his own ceremonies in advance, delivered his own urn for his ashes . . ."

"Ashes! Come on Pat, he hated fire, you know that."

"The war is past, Mike. He probably got over that phobia. So he opted for cremation. Besides, where the hell can they bury you in the city anymore?"

Getting turned back to pure dust again wasn't my idea of Dooley's mentality. Watching him the time we got trapped in a burning building with no way out made me realize how much he hated the kind of fire that could char you to shriveled, roasted meat. Somehow he'd opened a hole in the wall with a grenade, squeezed out and blasted the four enemy infantrymen who had cornered us and we had gotten back to our company without any trouble. It was months after that when Pat and I saw the rippled burn scars on his back while we were showering that it all made sense.

At her desk, Velda was dunking a bagel into her coffee cup. Pat walked over, saw the gimmick she had laid out on her blotter and mumbled around his hard roll, "What's that?"

"The latest in telephone bugs," she told him.

"Who'd give you guys an order to tap a phone?" We were good buddies, but he was still a cop.

For a minute we let him stew in it, then I said, "Nobody, pal. That was laid on us."

Velda tapped the desk phone in front of her. "This one."

"Nice," Pat said. "Who'd do that?"

I told him, "We know when, we know why, but we don't know who."

"Great. Now explain." He took another bite of his hard roll.

"That press conference was a pretty public affair. We only made a few calls and let them spread the word. Let's face it, me coming back all of a sudden was an interesting news item. Somebody who was at ease thinking I had been knocked off suddenly got the jumps to find out it hadn't happened. That one had an employee in the bunch that showed up here. Planting a bug would have been a snap during the interview when all eyes were focused on me."

"So?"

"So let me feel important, will you?"

Pat finished his roll and nodded. "Be my guest."

"By the way, how big a bundle would a million bucks in hundreds make?"

He looked at me like I was kidding, but my eyes said I wasn't.

"A big cardboard carton full. Clothes dryer size."

"Then a billion would take a thousand cartons like that."

Pat seemed puzzled now. "Yeah, why?"

I chose a smaller number for easier figuring. "Then how big a place would you need to store eighty thousand cartons that size?"

"Mike," he said, "getting shot has plain screwed up your mind."

"That's no answer."

"How about a great big warehouse, then?"

"That's what I figured." I grinned at him and said, "What would you do with a bundle that big, Pat?"

"Buy a new car," he growled, wondering what brought all this on.

"That is what I thought," I said, grinning at his answer.

Velda didn't get the exchange either and shook her head at us. "What do we do with the bug, Mike?"

"Can you put it back?"

"I took it off, didn't I? Only let's not use the same phone. This gadget is a miniature transmitter so it will work off any unit, except that it will transmit only what we want somebody to hear."

"Good," I said. "Do it."

While she inserted the bug into the phone on the other desk, Pat and I finished the goodies, had a last half cup of coffee and checked the time.

Downstairs we caught a cab over to Richmond's funeral parlor, saw DOOLEY neatly lettered in on a mahogany sign with an arrow pointing to the chapel on the left. The quietness that sat on these moneyed morgues was dank. Like a fog. Faces would go by dripping with grief or rigid with stoicism, determined to fight a terrible sorrow. Only the attendants seemed human. They were good at pretending grief or consolation, even when their shorts were too tight. But that was not out of place because somebody had to hold the pieces together.

I was expecting to find the place empty, but that wasn't the way it was at all. There must have been two dozen people there. Two were women. They were in a corner together talking softly and one was crying. Not much, but the grief showed. Most of the others were ordinary guys. They could have been workers who came out during their lunch hour or maybe neighbors of old Dooley. Four of them were gathered around a chest-high display table that held a graciously carved urn.

I knew what that was. Marcos Dooley was in there.

And the guy looking at me was wishing it was me instead. He was almost as tall as I was and from the way his six-hundred-dollar suit fit you knew he worked out on all the Nautilus equipment and most likely jogged fifty miles a week. He had the good looks of a Sicilian dandy and the composure of a Harvard graduate, but under that high-priced facade he was a street punk named Ponti. The *younger.*

I walked over to him. We had never met, but we didn't need an introduction. I said, "Hello. Come to pay your respects?"

Under his coat his muscles tightened and his eyes measured me. There was a wary tautness in the way he stood, ready for anything and hoping it would happen, and the sooner the better. He was like an animal, the young male in the prime of life and now he wanted to challenge the old bull. He knew that the longer nothing happened the less chance he had to win and an expectant anxiety showed in the lines around his mouth. He looked just like Drago and Patterson at Le Cirque.

I played the old bull's part perfectly. I said, "Your buddies left my calling card on their table. I took it back."

His eye twitched, so he wasn't as cool as he thought he was. "Oh?"

Real Harvard-like, I thought. "Tell them I'm saving it, Ugo."

His eyes flicked to see if anyone was listening. "I'll do that."

The old bull said, "You didn't answer my question."

"Dooley worked for my father."

"I know that." I got a frown again, strangely concerned this time.

"And how do you know him?"

"We were in the army together. So was that cop over there." Ugo didn't have to look. He knew who I meant. Pat was looking right at us. He got that twitch again and I knew the young buck had lost the confrontation. But there would be another time and the young buck would get stronger and the old bull would be aging out of the picture. He hoped.

At the display table, I got a close look at Dooley's encapsulation. It was a dulled metallic urn, modestly decorated at the top and bottom with a plaque in the middle engraved with gold lettering.

His name, age and birthplace were at the top, then under it a brief history that gave his GI serial numbers in eight digits and a record of his service aboard the U.S. destroyer *Latille.* Nothing about his army time at all. Hell, both Pat and I knew Dooley had come from someplace else he wouldn't speak about before he was attached to our outfit. Now we knew. He had served in, then ducked out of the U.S. Navy. The son of a gun probably got seasick and called it quits, but was patriotic enough to get right back into the mess with another combat unit.

The funeral director for Richmond's sidled up next to me and asked, "Can I see you a moment, Mr. Hammer?"

I nodded and followed him to the far side of the room. He stood there primly, wondering how to explain the situation. "When Mr. Dooley purchased our . . . accommodations, he asked that you see to his . . . remains."

"Be glad to," I told him. "What did he want done with them?"

"He said he had a son named Marvin and wanted you to find him and deliver his ashes in the urn to the boy."

"I never knew about a kid."

"Apparently he had one he never mentioned."

"Well," I said to him, "if that's what he wanted, that's what he gets. I sure owe him that much."

He looked at his watch. Half the crowd had signed the register and already left. The others would be out in a few minutes. "I'll box the urn for you and you can pick it up in my office."

The three of us left the parlor with Dooley in my arms, packed in a box like a specimen of some kind. Pat wanted to know what I was going to do with him and I told him there was a private repository for jars of dead people in Queens. You paid a lifetime fee and visitors could come see your remains in a niche on a concrete wall. Pat wanted to split the fee with me because of our past relationship, so I agreed and took Dooley home with me.

Women are strange people. They are inbred nesters, ready to make a home the minute they have the chance, cleaning and changing and stirring up dirt where none was at all. Velda was doing this right now. Not physically, but with her mind and eyes. Mine was a bachelor's apartment. You knew a man lived here. It was expensive, but it had no frills. The decorations had a masculine nature, all in good taste. But Male. Now that was being softened with feminine overtones. She had been here often enough, but now it was different.

When the inspection was finished she said almost casually, "When are you planning to marry me, Mike?"

"You in a hurry?"

"Like you couldn't believe."

"Then help me to finish this Dooley affair," I said. She sat down and I slid into the cushion next to her. I told her about Dooley's tying in with Lorenzo and what he had said about the dons. In a general way I described the discord in the families and what they were going to do with their funds. Right then she turned quickly, her eyes narrowed, and said, "Did you notice that little fat guy as we went into Dooley's area?"

"Grey double-breasted suit, pink shirt?"

"That's the one."

"What about him?"

"He was either a Treasury man or an IRS agent. Six months ago I covered a trial at the Kings County Courthouse in Brooklyn and he was a witness for the prosecution."

"What was he doing at the funeral home?"

"He was *watching*, Mike."

A little hiss seeped through my lips.

"What's happening?" she asked me.

"You sure about that guy? The fat guy?"

"About ninety percent," she stated. "Now tell me what's going on."

"The leaks have started, kitten. One of them got picked

up by Uncle Sam. The tax boys have a scent and they'll follow it all the way through."

"To what?"

"To where eighty-nine billion dollars are stashed." It was the first time I had mentioned the numbers to her and she opened her mouth in an expression of utter disbelief.

"Mike . . ."

"Don't play it down, kid. The annual take from California's biggest cash crop would knock your socks off."

"What crop is that?"

"Marijuana. Happy grass."

"Mike . . . you said billions. Each billion is a thousand million."

"Pat thought so too."

"Then you weren't kidding . . . ?"

"Not about something that big." I gave her hand a gentle squeeze of reassurance. "Right now they're looking for dinosaurs. There aren't any. All they can find are fossils. Interesting to look at, but that's all. The only one who could tell them about it is dead."

"You believed Dooley, didn't you?"

I agreed with her. I did believe Dooley, all right. He told me what he did with all that loot, but he didn't tell me where. How he did it was another matter. How *would* you move eighty thousand cartons of pure, spendable cash and valuables in a way that was totally sight unseen? It was like watching Karloff in *The Mummy* when he was buried alive beside the lady who cheated on her husband. To keep the grave secret all the slaves were killed by the soldiers.

I always wondered what happened to the soldiers. They had sworn loyalty to the pharaoh so they were considered beyond suspicion of acting traitorously. At least until a stronger pharaoh came on the scene.

I shook the thought out of my head and stood up. "Tomorrow I want you to go down to the Veterans Administration and run down Dooley's service record." I scanned the serial numbers on the urn and wrote them down, handing the slip to Velda.

"What am I looking for?"

"His kid. He's supposed to have a son. All that information would have been recorded when he signed up."

"Where do I look first?"

"Try Washington, D.C. Use the phone. If they want any reason for the query, tell them we're trying to find an inheritor."

"Fine, Mike . . . but why *are* we looking for him?"

"Because fathers with sons are funny. They'll entrust things to their kids they wouldn't put in a safe deposit box. That kid, Marvin, may know something we need." After a moment I added, "One more thing. Check your calendar and see when you went to the Kings County Courthouse. Find out who that government witness was. You have any friends over there?"

"The best. The court stenographer. It's all public information anyway, but she can expedite matters."

When I didn't come up with something else, Velda folded the slip into her wallet then locked that in her purse. Her eyes came up to mine again, nice clear, deep brown, hungry eyes that didn't push or play games. She said, "That's for tomorrow. What's for tonight?"

"Kitten," I said, "you really know how to twist my tail. Now listen to me one more time. If you want to get married to me, you're going to do it the old-fashioned way. We can hold hands and kiss and hug all you want, but we keep our clothes on and stay out of bed. Got it?"

"Did that doctor . . . do anything to you, Mike?"

"Yeah. He kept me alive so that soon enough I *can* do

anything. One round with you under the sheets and I'll be on a slab."

With a tiny smile she said, "What a prude. He can brace two tough guys with no gun and one bullet and can't make love to his fiancée."

"Just following doctor's orders, sweetie."

"Mike," she said, "I wouldn't have it any other way."

The building was simple, wasting no space. It was concrete, boxlike, with a minimum of ornamentation, a cemetery supermarket where urns could be placed to be seen in delicately formed mini-caves pressed into the cement or hidden behind inch-thick facades with histories worked into their surfaces.

Marshall Brotorrio toured me through the lower recesses of the modern crypt knowing that would be all the inspection I would need. Since Dooley would not be getting many visitors he suggested the last niche on the row. I went along with that, opted to keep the urn in view, then went back to his office to complete the paperwork.

Dooley was still sitting on his desk, but somebody had cleaned and polished the metal container while we were away, slipping a plastic shield over it to keep fingertips from spotting its beauty.

"Would you like to see the urn placed in its resting place?"

The words didn't seem right coming from a big guy like Brotorrio. I shook my head. "I'm not much on ceremony."

"I understand," he said. And he did. An old pal burying his buddy after carrying his remains from one borough to another wasn't going to go all teary-eyed at this stage. I made out the check, signed the papers, shook hands with Marshall Brotorrio and went back to flag down a cab.

Now I had to find Dooley's son and pass over the papers to him, then find the slob who had iced Dooley.

I looked out the window and watched the skyline of New York coming up. From three miles out it looked clean and angular, but the closer you got the grayer the color was and the duller the angles seemed to be. At one point I got a momentary glimpse of the prettiest building in the city, the old Woolworth Building. It used to be the tallest in the world, but now it was dwarfed by the steel and glass structures that entombed the mighty organizations that breathed life in and out of great populations. I had only a brief peek, but it was nice to know the old lady was still there.

Velda got back to the office a few minutes after me. She watched while I downed two capsules Dr. Morgan had given to me. I had to flip them into an already-chewed cracker to get them down, but taking pills had never been one of my strong points. When I put the cap back on the plastic bottle I asked, "Well?"

She flipped open a small notebook and scanned it. "Our fat man is a Treasury agent, all right. Just where he stands in the pecking order, my friend couldn't tell me, but he's way up there. She called him a *funny money sniffer.* Whenever the government suspects a person or organization of holding back big tax funds, Homer Watson is called in."

"Homer Watson?"

"I know," she said, "sounds like a country boy, but he broke the Fintel scandal and nailed those Wall Street insiders who almost took a billion dollars home to mama." Velda was watching me closely now. "That story you gave to Pat was real, wasn't it?"

After a few seconds I shrugged. "I don't know. Nothing's been proven. It's only what I've been told."

"But you believe it," she stated flatly.

"Yes," I said. "I believe it."

"Why?"

"Because I went through a war with the guy who told me."

"A real man thing, I suppose."

"You suppose right, kitten. Why the interrogation?"

"I want to believe it too and it scares me. Will you answer me one question?"

"Sure," I agreed.

For a moment she stood there, thinking silently, then said, "Eighty-nine billion dollars is an almost impossible amount of money. There is no way a person could spend it all. Governments or individuals would gladly kill to pull in numbers like that, and there are organizations and persons who have the financing and technology to search out a treasure that big."

I nodded and told her, "That's not the question, doll."

"True," she agreed. Then: "How are you going to beat them all to it?"

My laugh was almost a grunt. "I'm smart," I said.

"Don't give me that." Now a frown had started between her eyes. "You can have the entire government of the United States on your back just like that."

"So?"

"How are you going to handle *that*?"

"No problem," I said.

"Oh, great."

"Come on, Velda, I can't tell them what I don't know."

"What did Dooley tell you?" she asked me shrewdly.

"Not enough."

"You knew the amount."

"Sure, but not where it *was*. I think Dooley wanted to

tell me, but all he said was that he had changed the signs so *nobody* could find it."

"Why do you suppose he called you in, Mike?"

Now I grinned real big. "Because I'm not *nobody*. Somehow Dooley dropped it right in my lap and now I have to look down at all the wrinkles in the napkin to see where the crumb is. That'll tell me where it is."

"And what do you do with eighty-nine billion dollars after you find it?"

"Same thing Pat would do. I'd buy a new car. Hell, you can have some too. New dress, shoes, things like that."

"Get serious," Velda told me.

"I am," I said. "Now, what about Dooley's history?"

The change of pace rattled her for a moment, then she thumbed over another page of her notebook. For a moment she frowned at it, then her eyes drifted up to mine. "Those navy serial numbers were wrong, Mike. They weren't his."

Before I could answer her she cut me off with a wave of her hand. "Oh, I found him, all right. I ran down the personnel on the destroyer *Latille*, and there he was. Then I got his proper ID. I had to mention a few names to get his son's name and addresses, but I knew you wouldn't mind." She ripped a page out of the notepad and handed it to me. "Anyway, there's the kid's location as far as they know."

I looked at the address, memorized it and tucked the paper under my desk blotter. "We still have a problem, kitten."

She waited for me to say it.

"What are those other numbers on the urn then?"

"Maybe . . ." she searched for a name, then found it, "Marvin can tell you."

A little nerve tugged at my jaw. Dooley had always been

out front with everything. He had wanted to bust right into a bunker rather than smoke an enemy out. He never seemed to be devious with anything, so it was hard to give him credit for it now. Hell, he *could* have made a mistake, but that sure didn't seem likely. Nobody *ever* forgets his military serial number. Nobody. Ever. You don't forget where to wear your hat either. Or put your socks.

So? Okay, Dooley was trying to be devious. Oh boy, if those numbers were a code to all that loot and the government picked it up, their computers could break it in ten seconds. Maybe five. And the mob had the same technology too. So where did that leave me? I looked at Velda's face and knew that she was thinking the same thing, picturing all those beautiful IBM machines and supercomputers and assorted goodies lined up in the government offices in Washington, making subtle clicking sounds, churning out reams of information all generated by a steady current of electricity smug with its power.

"They're only as good as what people put into them, Mike," she offered.

"Yeah," I agreed.

She smiled a little sweetly, then tested me. "What's better than a computer virus, Mike?"

But I knew the answer. "When they don't know what to feed them."

Velda had left early, trying to expedite locating Marvin Dooley. It was almost five, no new business had come in and I was ready to close up shop. I heard the two short buzzes in Velda's office and hit the door button to let the visitor in.

It was the little fat man from Washington, affable, well dressed and seemingly on a happy errand rather than one that would necessitate a visit to a private investigator's office. All I could think was, *I am from the government and am here to help you.*

"Well," I said, "Mr. Homer Watson, I presume."

That took his breath away a little. The upturned corners of the false smile turned down and the affable look just wasn't there anymore. "Sharp, Mr. Hammer. It didn't take you long."

"It never does, pal."

"You know why I'm here?"

"Certainly," I said. I nodded to a chair and sat down myself, the desk a barrier between us.

My approach had gotten him unfocused, something that probably never happened before.

"And what would that be?" he asked.

I didn't let him off the hook. "I take it you're not here to ask for my professional help, are you?"

We were fencing now. "Oh. I'll pay it," he told me easily.

"You'd be lost in the rush, Mr. Watson."

I still hadn't asked him what he wanted and he was doing a mental search to make his point known. Annoyed, he said, "How did you know my name?"

"I'm a detective. State licensed. Can carry a weapon and all that kind of stuff, you know?"

"Yeah, I know," he told me tartly. "Please don't be a smart ass."

"Okay, then tell me why you're here."

"A call was made to Washington by your secretary. The subject party had been red flagged and the information was passed on to me."

"So?"

His face reddened. "What did you want to know about him?"

Now I put the hook in deeper. "You carry a badge?"

"Yes."

"Let me see it. And the other credentials too."

Homer Watson was really teed off now, but he dug out his badge and photo ID and passed it over. I took a minute scrutinizing it then handed it back. "You have a warrant?"

"No," he admitted.

"That's bad," I said. "Then this is just a normal business meeting, right?"

Rather than answer, he frowned, trying to get around the situation.

Finally I let him off the hook. I grinned and said, "What do you want to know about Dooley and the mob, Homer?"

He looked at me for ten seconds, then shook his head in mock disgust. "I should have listened to the street talk when they tried to tell me about you."

I nodded knowingly.

"What was your connection with Dooley?"

"We were in the army together. After the war he steered Pat Chambers and me into police work."

"How did you know he was connected with the mob?"

"I didn't."

"But . . ."

"He mentioned he had done some work for one of the families, but hell, so have I. So have a lot of people, but that doesn't mean he was connected to the mob. Dooley and I have been out of touch for a long time."

"Yet he called for you when he was dying."

"He had to call for somebody. His wife was dead and he probably didn't know where his kid lived. He wanted me to pass on his remains to his boy if I could find him. Why, what do you think he wanted to see me for?"

"It could have been a deathbed confession."

"Come on, Dooley had no part of religion. He lost that during the war. Do I look like a clergyman?"

"He could have been entrusting you with some vital information."

I leaned back in my chair and let a grimace cross my face. "Like what? When Dooley died he left an old house in a shoddy side of Brooklyn. There was an old car out back. If he had a bank account there wouldn't be much in it. Possessing things wasn't his big stick."

"He had a long-time connection with the Ponti organization, Mr. Hammer."

"Like how, Mr. Watson? Damn, I sound like Sherlock Holmes."

"Dooley took care of his estate on Long Island and his place in the Adirondacks."

"Big deal. He was a handyman. He raked grass, he planted shrubs and took out the garbage. How does that make him an associate member of the Ponti bunch? Come on, use some sense."

"He could have overheard things."

Watson was reaching now, so I reached too. I said, "What things, Homer?"

"You know what I'm talking about."

"Like how all the young bucks in the families are grousing about their futures?"

A new light came into his eyes. "What would that be?"

"Beats me, but I hear a lot of them are pretty uncomfortable with all the legitimizing that has been going on. Seems like the old dons had a better life of it when they played dirty."

He couldn't put a finger on my answer at all. What I had said was totally ambiguous, yet common knowledge on the street. Yet in a way, it had sense to it and he tried to read something into my expression.

Covering his consternation, he nodded. "The new heads of the families are all looking for something."

"They ought to be. It's a new business world out there. It isn't booze and whores anymore. It's high-tech crime on airline loading docks and the financial houses of Wall Street. They buy a plane to run in one big load of coke, ditch it after making the drop and charge the cost off to business expenses. A kilo of H used to be a heavy deal, but narcotics comes in tonnages now and who knows how much loot gets passed under the table."

"We estimate it pretty well, Mr. Hammer."

Lightly, I said, "And how much would that be?"

Just as lightly he shot back, "Could go into the billions, I imagine."

"Imagine the taxes on that," I said.

"Yes, and the government could use it," he told me. There was a sharp tone in his voice.

"What would they do with it?" I asked him.

"I don't think that would be any of your business, Mr. Hammer."

"We, the people," I said softly.

He didn't hear me. "What?"

"Nothing. I figured you'd say that."

The conversation wasn't giving him what he was looking for at all. He eased himself to his feet and looked at me across the desk. "I think we both have the same objective in mind, Mr. Hammer. I would prefer your cooperation, but I don't think I'm going to get it. However, please keep in mind the enormous potential of the federal government. There's nothing it can't do."

"Don't make it so complete, Homer. Say there's *little* it can't do."

He stared at me a few seconds and said, "Let's make that as little as possible."

When Watson had gone I sat back in my chair and stared out the window. The sky had clouded over, so that meant it was going to rain and my side was going to start burning again. Before it could happen I thumbed open the bottle of capsules and shook one out. Good lunch. A saltine and a pill. At the rate I was taking those things I was going to need a refill, and Dr. Ralph Morgan was the only one who had the prescription. I made a cryptic note on my desk pad for later.

First I had to find out something about Bulletproof Ponti. Pat's earlier remarks on the two shoot-outs had a casual overtone to them, but he was using me as a sounding board and I hadn't made much of an echo. It used to be that only the big agency teams or the SWAT boys went into a firefight wearing armor. The hoods seemed to wear their macho image the way the Indians used magic medicine to ward off the bullets and always got sucked up the tube for their egotism.

But now, things had changed. They didn't use old hard-tire trucks to haul their goods in. Planes did that. Ground rules might have been laid down during the prohibition days, but there had been a lot of improvement since. Even in the last five years body armor had undergone a radical transformation. Planes went from reciprocating engines to jet driven overnight. They still had wings, but the power had been so drastically upgraded they hardly acted like airplanes anymore.

I dialed a number I hadn't used in a long time. Bud Langston was still at the address. He was really glad to hear my voice.

Bud was a super secret whose mail-in paycheck came from some bureau in the Washington loop. His office was small, well organized and laid out for his business, which was computer programming. Any one of the major electronics firms would gladly have had him in their organizations, but Bud was not into *corporate living.*

Bud Langston was an inventor. Tell him what you needed and he'd invent it for you. We had met when we had adjoining seats for a Wagner presentation at the old Metropolitan Opera House before they tore it down and all the singers trooped over to Lincoln Center.

So we sat and talked Wagner and Franz Liszt for a half hour before Bud said, "What's bothering you, Mike?"

I grimaced, twisted in my seat and favored the bad side.

Bud shook his head. "That's not what's bothering you, my friend."

"I need some information, Bud."

His eyes looked directly into mine. "If it isn't classified I might help."

"If it were redlined I wouldn't ask," I said. "Have you heard anything new about body armor?"

"Let's skip past the Kevlar developments, right?"

"Right," I said.

A little muscle pulled at the corner of his mouth, making him grin a little lopsidedly. "Well, that's not classified."

"I didn't think it would be."

He nodded slowly and clasped his hands behind his head. "You sure can get into some strange research, Mike."

"So?"

"So yes, there was a buzz in the armaments business a few years ago. Remember when the scuba divers were experimenting with a metal mesh designed after the old chain mail the knights used?"

"For stopping shark bites, wasn't it?"

"Yes, and it worked. At least on smaller sharks. Nobody ever tested it out on a great white."

"And that stopped high-power bullets?"

"No. That experimentation just led into other avenues and along the way somebody lucked into a material that nothing short of a twenty-millimeter could penetrate. It was *light,* flexible . . . all the things needed for *military* use. The only trouble was the expense."

"Why didn't the military get into it then?"

"Mike . . . there won't be any military in the next war."

I waited. My mind kept bringing back episodes from the war I was in. Bud seemed to know what I was thinking and shook his head.

"Those old wars were too expensive. They didn't solve anything. The bad guys and the good guys just swapped sides, that's all. The wall came down, Russia fell, Africa came apart and the military industrial complex is simply getting rid of its surplus hardware. What happens next is going to be biological and chemical with no noise and no blood. Just death. Ugly, destructive death."

"Who gets what's left?" I asked him.

"Who belongs to the big country clubs?" he fired back.

"And that's the plan?"

Bud said, "I think it's their plan."

"You think it'll work?"

"Hell, no. There are a lot of people smarter than big governments. But what's all this have to do with body armor?"

"Who invented it, Bud?"

"A young chemistry whiz two years out of some university. His name is Dan Coulter. He manufactured enough product to demonstrate to the government, but everybody balked at the price and he peddled it somewhere else."

"He patent it?"

"No way. He kept his process strictly secret, and now nobody is ever going to find out how he did it."

"Why not?"

"Because his whole place blew up with him in it. Dan Coulter is dead."

"Damn," I said.

"Before you ask, there was nothing suspicious about the blast. He was using some very critical materials. It's a wonder he got as far as he did."

"One more question, Bud."

"Sure."

"Could you *duplicate* his work?"

"Certainly," he said amicably, "but not right now. Living is still a pleasant way to be."

"What are you hinting at, Bud?"

"Two of his *suppliers* are both dead too. They were involved with his work."

"How?"

"Separate car accidents three weeks apart. Suspiciously accidental."

I eased myself into a standing position. "You knew this Coulter guy, didn't you?"

"Both of us belonged to diving clubs."

"You said you could duplicate his work."

"There's no reason to."

"Supposing I'd like to see what the stuff looks like."

"In that case then I'll get a sample and show it to you."

"Why do I have to drag everything out of you, Bud?"

"I'm just giving you back some of your own medicine, kiddo. Stop by in about a week and I'll put on a show for you."

THERE ARE THINGS some people can get done on a telephone that seem incredible, but when you analyze it, the whole affair is simple, direct and logical. It had taken a hour for Velda to locate Marvin Dooley's latest address on the outskirts of New Brunswick and find out it was a single-room apartment in a run-down section of the city. He had been there for three months, coming from Trenton, was self-employed, had a driver's license, but no car was registered in his name. I left a call on her answering machine to be ready at four so I could pick her up and beat the rush out of Manhattan.

And she was ready, all right, but just as ready to start up all over again about us not carrying beepers so we could have a more immediate contact. I closed the car door on her, went around to the driver's side and climbed in. I slid the key into the slot and was about to turn the ignition on when I looked down the hood line and stopped.

Velda caught my reaction right away and drew in her breath. "What is it, Mike?"

After a moment I asked, "What is it you don't like about my vehicle, kitten?"

"You're a slob. It's always dirty."

"Uh-huh."

I picked the keys back out, put the gear lever in neutral and told her to get out of the car and stand around the corner.

"Why?"

"Because somebody squeezed in between the car and the wall to open the hood and left a big clean spot on the metal."

"You think you have a bomb under there?"

"Somebody did something."

"Then call Pat and let him get the squad over here."

"If I'm wrong I'll be using up brownie points. If I'm right I'll have the DA's office under my feet again."

"Mike . . . are you looking to get dead?"

"No. Now get around the corner like I told you."

"Up yours, boss. You die, I die. They'll have to give us a double funeral. After all this time I'm not letting you off the hook so easy."

"Swell. Then start pushing the car back a couple of feet."

I had unlocked the hood latch from inside the car, the same way they did. I slid the lever over, pulled the hood up and shone a flashlight down into the engine compartment. There was no attempt to hide the unit, a simple arrangement hooked to the ignition for a power source, but this time there wasn't a bundle of dynamite sticks, but a one-inch-by-four-inch foil-wrapped charge carefully selected for its destructive capabilities. Whoever installed it seemed very sure of himself. There was no booby trap device, no motion igniting mechanism, just that little packet of death waiting for the turn of a key to turn us into red splashes and pieces of flesh.

I unhooked the ignition contact and lifted out the charge. Velda looked around the parking area and said, "What would that have done . . . to all this, Mike?"

I knew she was thinking about the bombing of the Towers downtown. "It wouldn't be like that, kitten. This would have wiped us out along with the cars on both sides and left a lot of soot on this level." I grinned at her. "We'd be like red graffiti."

"You're disgusting, Mike."

"Watch it, doll, we're not married yet."

I wrapped the wires around the foil package and slid it under the driver's seat. Velda gave me an incredulous look. "You're not taking that thing with you . . . are you?"

"It isn't the kind of explosive that goes off with normal impact. You can squeeze it, hit it, stomp on it . . . but just don't toss it in the fireplace or jolt it with an electrical spark."

She finally asked, "Who did it, Mike?"

"The orders probably came from Ponti the Younger. The old man's too smart to be this obvious. Lorenzo doesn't play the emotion game. There's more at stake than that. He'll want to know what *he thinks* I know before he makes any move on me."

"And what would that be?"

"Whatever Dooley told me." I looked over at her, my eyes narrowing in a frown. "And that is relatively nothing," I added.

I turned the key and the engine purred into life. It was a heck of a way to find out, but there were no slimy seconds under the hood to cover for a misfire. I backed out of the slot and cranked the wheel over and went up the ramp to the street. If anybody was watching, they'd most likely swear under their breath and take it out on their supplier of military goodies.

Velda had charted the run to New Brunswick right on the nose. There were no wrong turns, no stopping to ask directions, just a straight, easy drive. When I stopped in front of the decrepit old building where Marvin Dooley lived, she said, "You like my navigation?"

I grinned. "Beautiful, kitten. I hope you can cook like that."

The place had a common vestibule that housed eight mailboxes, a single overhead bulb and the smell of multiracial cooking. The slots beneath the mailboxes held names, except for one, and since Dooley wasn't in any of the others, that blank one had to be Marvin's. I pushed the button and tried the door. It swung open with no trouble. Muted TV voices overlapped in the area and somewhere a radio was tuned in to a rock station that thumped out a monotonous beat. Behind me, Velda closed the door.

To our left was a wooden staircase leading to the second level. A door creaked open, feet clicked across the floorboards and a male voice yelled over the banister, "Yeah, whatta ya want?"

"Marvin?"

There was a moment's hesitation before he answered, "Who wants him?"

But by then I was up the stairs and his head jerked around, not knowing whether to hold his ground or duck back into his room. "I'm Mike Hammer, Marvin. I was in the army with your father."

"He's dead."

"We know."

"Who's *we*?"

Just then Velda came up the stairs and took his breath away long enough for him to lose his antagonistic attitude. "We are more people than you could imagine," I said quietly. "You mind inviting us inside?"

He glanced at me a few seconds, frowned, then stared at Velda long enough to change his mind and nodded toward the door. I waited for him to go in first, followed him in closely, then waved to Velda to come and close the door.

As I expected it was a nothing place. One room with a cot that doubled as a sofa, a two-burner stove, small sink and a narrow old-fashioned refrigerator that took up a corner. The kitchen table had two wooden chairs and an old canvas beach chair was right in front of a fairly new TV that was set on the floor. But at least it was clean. There were no dirty dishes, no dust accumulation, no pile of clothes and the only lingering smell was that of an antiseptic soap.

He caught my thoughts right away and said, "I'm poor but neat, Mr. Hammer." His eyes shifted to Velda and he added, "No woman's here, lady. It was something I picked up in the navy."

"The lady is my associate," I told him. "Her name is Velda."

No surprise showed in his expression. He nodded toward her and said, "The piece in the paper mentioned her. At the funeral."

"Why weren't you there, Marvin?"

He shrugged eloquently. "What good would that have done?"

I knew what he meant. "You didn't miss anything. He was just ashes in a metal vase."

"Who came to see him off?"

"Just people who knew him in the old days. Some others he worked for. Not too many."

"That mob bunch, huh?"

"Somebody had to cut their grass," I said.

"Baloney. If my old man did that he was playing a game."

"Marvin . . . how would you know? When was the last time you saw your father?"

"Before I went in the navy. We hardly kept in touch. A couple of letters and a card that gave me his new address." A touch of shrewdness seemed to touch his eyes and he looked directly at me. "What did the old man leave me, Mr. Hammer?"

"An urn full of ashes, kiddo. What did you expect?"

"Don't give me that crap, buster. You didn't come all the way down here to tell me that. He left me something and you need me to get it."

"I need you like a hole in the head," I said. I took out my notepad and wrote down a name and address, then handed it to him. "All your father wanted was for me to get in touch with you. I took his ashes and put them in a repository. This is where they are. Do what you want with them."

The shrewdness seemed to seep out of his eyes. He fingered the paper, mouthing the address silently. He finally looked up at me. "That's all?"

"That is all."

He studied me again, his teeth grating at his lips. "You said you were in the army with my father."

"That's right."

"He was in the navy," he challenged.

I nodded. "We found that out when Velda contacted the Veterans Bureau in Washington."

"How the hell did he get in the army? Damn, that

doesn't make sense. All the old man ever wanted was to get out on the ocean."

"He ever do that?"

"Not before he joined the navy. All he ever did was run that old boat of his up and down the Hudson River."

That was something Dooley had never mentioned to us at all. In all the tight pockets we had been in, when going over details of your lifetime with your buddies in the same foxhole kept the tension down and the awareness high, never had Dooley told us about a boat. His old Rollfast bicycle, the Flexible Flier sled, the Union Hardware roller skates, those things we knew. But nothing about a boat.

"What kind of a boat?" I asked him.

He ran it through his head trying to determine its importance, then figuring it had none, said, "A Woolsey."

The name didn't mean anything to me. "What did it look like?"

"Hey, boats aren't my thing, Hammer. It was pretty old. He was always repairing the wood, kind of like it was his hobby."

"He ever take it out?"

"Sure. Like when the weather was right. He didn't trust the boat enough to get into any rough water. Most of the time he went up and down the river."

"You ever go with him?"

"When I was a kid, sure. I didn't like it though. That was his bag, not mine."

I had to keep probing into this little side venture of Dooley's. "He have any special places to tie up?"

"Nah. He'd just cruise around and tell me how he always wanted to get out to sea. If we stopped it was to gas up or grab a sandwich."

"Then where did you go to?"

Marvin gave me an annoyed smirk. "Where can you go

on the Hudson? Twice we got as far as Albany. Big deal. Most of the time we'd go north to Poughkeepsie or south below Bear Mountain. If I started to get sick he'd head for home."

"Where was that?"

"A little old marina a few miles north of Newburgh. Nothing much there now, but back in the old days there were about a dozen yachts docked."

"You know who owns it?"

"Come on, I was a kid then. Some old man had it. He must have been eighty, so he's probably dead now." He paused and his head jerked around so he could look straight at me. "You didn't answer my question."

"Your old man wasn't a deserter, Marvin. He just traded in being a lousy sailor for a damn good soldier. Either way, he volunteered. All he did was beat the paperwork."

Again, I got a hard stare. "And you came all the way down here to tell me where his ashes are?"

"Only because your father left those instructions."

Knowingly, he asked, "What else?"

"To find out if you could tell me any details that could have gotten him shot."

"You should do better than that, Mr. Hammer." I waited and let him add the rest himself. "He was killed for a reason. He was a nobody. There wasn't any property except his house, he didn't have a big job, he didn't get into any trouble, but *something* got him murdered. He didn't get killed accidental-like."

"I think this was an accident waiting a long time to happen," I said. "You know any of his friends at all?"

"Nah. I never knew he had any. The only one I ever saw him around was old Harris."

"Who?"

"Some old swampie they called Slipped Disk Harris."

"Who?"

Velda answered me from across the room. "He was a bootlegger back in the prohibition days. They say he got his name from tossing too many cases of illegal whiskey into trucks."

"Now how would you know that?" I demanded.

"I read a lot," she told me. "Want more?"

"Yeah," I said, "I want more."

"Fine. He was very successful, always a great supplier, never got caught and became very rich. He was alleged to have been a *made man,* but that was never proven. However, he *did* have a great deal of influence with known big-time racketeers."

I looked at Marvin. "That sound like him?"

Velda's recitation had left him with a surprised expression. "Yeah," he agreed, "that was him, all right. He holed up with the old man a couple of times when some of the guys were after his tail."

"Why?"

Marvin gave a casual shrug. "What it sounded like to me was that Slipped Disk was still selling booze down in the big city, but his prices knocked the regular retailers to hell and gone."

"Look, you're talking about a time long after prohibition. Hijacking went out of style when they brought the U.S. government down on them."

I got another shrug. "So who knows. I was only a little kid. I just remember them laughing about it."

"You think your father was in on it?"

"My old man? Get outa here. He couldn't be bothered getting into big business. All he wanted was to play it day by day. Now look what happens. He's a handyman for mobsters and he gets gunned down like an informer. For what? Nothing, that's what." Marvin rubbed his hands over his face, then ran his fingers through his hair. "You want anything else?" he asked.

"Would you give it to me if I did?"

"Depends."

I handed him one of my old cards Velda had put in my pocket. "Just one thing, Marvin."

"Oh?"

"Your father was killed for a reason. Whoever did it might think he entrusted information to you and—"

"He didn't tell me nothing! He—"

"I know that and you know that, but the killer is up in the air so there's a possibility that the quicker we get that guy the longer you'll have to live. Give it a thought, Marvin."

I took Velda's arm and steered her toward the door. When she reached the downstairs entrance she stopped and her hand slid under her coat. I knew she had her hand on the butt of the .38 she carried and reached out and grabbed her wrist. Darkness had settled in and we were in a strange area where security was null and patrol cars rarely cruised by.

"Nobody followed us," I told her.

"Mike, you've been in bad shape . . ."

"Nothing's happened to my instincts, doll. After that bomb bit I kept my eyes open." I stepped out onto the stoop, checked both ways and waved for Velda to come on. The car was still there, nobody had scratched it, kicked it or dented it. And the tiny bit of paper was still in the door hinge as a telltale.

"Clean," I said.

"Why don't you check under the hood anyway?"

I got the flashlight out, popped open the hood and inspected around the motor. "See, clean," I said. We got in, I inserted the key and turned the engine on. There was no explosion and we both let our breaths out at the same time.

"Damn it, Mike, you were expecting something!" Velda charged.

This time my laugh was real. And relieved.

The traffic flow on the Jersey Turnpike was loose and fast, so we got back to the city early enough for me to drop Velda off at her apartment and let me change shirts at mine. I didn't want her where I had to go and before I put on my jacket I went back on what I had told Pat.

I was going to see Don Lorenzo Ponti and all the odds were going to be on his side. But in these games of going face-to-face, I didn't want to start looking like a pathetic slob hoping for a handout. Ponti was getting old, but the game stayed the same. I got out my old shoulder holster, slipped into it, put a clip of fresh ammo in the .45 and tucked it in the leather. It rode in a bad spot and hurt like mad, but after a few adjustments it felt better even if it sat where a quick draw wasn't likely.

All I hoped was that the boneheads Ponti kept around him had good memories and better imaginations.

The local club was straight out of an old television movie. *No class* had been deliberately set in 1920's brick and concrete, with building blocks of translucent glass to let in light on the main floor while keeping anybody from seeing in. The nondescript stores flanking the club were owned by Ponti, but kept unoccupied to protect the club itself. The only thing different was that no graffiti artists had touched a spray can of paint to the concrete.

I got out of the cab a half block away and let them see me walk up to the club. There were two hoods outside the door who came out of the same TV show as the building and for a few seconds it looked like they were going to move right in on me, then one hood whispered something, the other seemed puzzled, then his face went blank.

I walked too fast for them to try to flank me, one on either side, and grinned at their consternation at suddenly being vulnerable if any shooting started. To make sure they stayed that way I ran my fingers under the brim of my pork pie and knew they both had a good look at the butt end of the gun on my side.

You don't try to be nice to guys like this. I said, "Go tell your boss I want to talk to him."

"He ain't here," the fat one said.

"Want me to shoot the lock off?" I didn't make it sound like a question.

Thinking wasn't something either one of these two was good at. They sure knew who I was but couldn't get the picture at all. The fat one tried to snarl and said to his partner, "Why don't you go get Lenny, Teddy."

"If that's Leonard Patterson, tell him I still have a present he didn't pick up."

The guy called Teddy said, "You got a big mouth, mister."

"I got a big name too, Teddy boy. It's Mike Hammer and you remember it. Now shake your tail and do what your buddy told you to do." And the look I got was what I wanted. That Teddy character was going to be another snake to look out for. He sure didn't buy being put down in front of a punk like the fat boy.

Leonard Patterson didn't come out alone. Howie Drago was right beside him and a big nickel-plated revolver dangled from his right hand. The game was still going strong because the other players still didn't know the rules. Hell, they didn't even know what game it was. What was on their faces wasn't puzzlement. They'd look like that if they were halfway across the Atlantic Ocean in a canoe and a storm was brewing.

You don't let them talk first either. "You going to take me to see the don or do I go up alone?"

Howie reacted first. "He's carrying, Patti."

"And I got a license for it, kiddo. You got one of those?"

"You're not coming in here wearing a rod, Hammer."

I didn't get to answer him. The dark figure leaning over the banister upstairs yelled down in his softly accented voice, "What's going on down there?"

Once again I beat the pair to the punch. "It's Mike Hammer," I called back. "If you don't want to talk to me, I'll beat it. If you want trouble I'll shoot the hell out of your guys here and the cops can mop up the mess."

I think the dialogue came out of that TV movie too.

"He's got a gun on him, Mr. Ponti," Patterson yelled.

"In his hand?"

"No. It's under his coat."

Ponti was like a cat. His curiosity was as tight as a stretched rubber band. He didn't even wait a second before he said, "He's always got that gun. Let him come on up, unless you want to shoot it out down there."

Ponti was a player, all right. Two old school kids were meeting on the dirty playground to duke it out and the rest of the gang could go kiss their tails. When I got to the top of the stairs Ponti just nodded for me to follow him and he walked in front of me as if it were all one big tea party. He could have been showing off or he could have men hidden waiting for me to jump him, but there was no fear in his movements at all. He pushed through a door to an office, but I didn't go through. I made sure the door flattened against the wall so nobody was behind it, visually scanned the area, then stepped in and edged along the wall to a chair in front of Ponti's desk.

His expression seemed to appreciate my cautiousness. "Are you nervous, Mr. Hammer?"

"Just careful."

"You take big chances."

"Not really."

"Oh?"

"I could have blown those goons you have downstairs right out of their socks if they tried to play guns."

"You could lose. There were a lot of them."

"I've been there before," I reminded him.

A hardness flushed his face. "Yes. I know."

For thirty seconds I just stood there staring at him, then moved around the chair and sat down. "Go ahead and ask it," I said.

The don played his role magnificently. He pulled his leather padded desk chair back on its rollers, sat down easily and folded his hands in his lap. It was taking an effort, but he was keeping his face in repose. When he was ready his eyes met mine and he said, "Did you kill my son, Mr. Hammer?"

There was no waiting this time either. "I shot him right in the head, Don Ponti. He had put two into me and was about to give me one right in the face when I squeezed a .45 into his head. You're damn right I shot him and if you have any more like him who want to try that action on me I'll do the same thing again."

I didn't know what to expect, certainly not the look of calm acceptance he wore. He seemed to be mentally reviewing the details of that night and when all the pieces fit into the puzzle he seemed oddly satisfied. "I do not blame you, Mr. Hammer," he told me quietly. "Of course, the public does not know what really happened, do they?"

"I wasn't around for any discussion."

"No, to them it was a gang war. The police were quite willing to let it go at that."

"What was it, Mr. Ponti?" I asked.

"A gang war," he told me amicably. "They happen, you know."

"Not like that. Not when the businesses are going along smoothly and the boss of bosses can take a vacation. Not when some of them who were shot up during the battle didn't belong there to start with. There was no street talk about a rumble about to happen and if you hadn't taken the normal precautions you would have been a total casualty when it was over."

"Taking precautions has kept me alive," he said, "but tell me, why were *you* there at all?"

"Because I had been tipped off that it was going down. The tip wasn't from any organization. It came from a drunk who overheard a couple of guys talking. I got it very casually, but it didn't take long to figure out it was damn real and if you didn't get hit, you could put a finger right on me for setting something up."

"That's not your style, is it?"

"No, but I don't know how *you* think."

"Would you like to know how I think?"

"Sure," I said.

Ponti told me, "I think ya got some kind of a con going here. So you told me about shooting Azi, but he asked for that himself. He's dead now and that's that. You want something from me then say it. What're you looking for?"

"I want whoever killed Marcos Dooley."

A sudden frown struck his forehead. "Dooley was a-nice-a man," he said, the accent coming back. "I don't know why anybody would want to kill him. He was a man of the soil, a gardener. For a long time he worked on my estates."

"Yeah, I know."

"Then why did he die, Mr. Hammer?"

"Somebody thought he knew more than he should."

"What *could* he know?"

"He mentioned trouble in your organization, Don Ponti."

"There is no trouble. Everything has been legal for years."

"Screw the legalities. It's the distribution of wealth that causes a ruckus."

"Do I look like a rich man, Mr. Hammer?"

"Cut the crap, don. You're one of the last real actors. I know you got all the land and the big houses when the prices were right in the old days, and your stable of cars is old, but expensively foreign. You still eat pasta and your clothes are tailored by an old man in your own neighborhood. So you don't *look* right. It fools a lot of people."

"Not the IRS."

"Like they say, creative bookkeeping takes care of that."

He just looked at me with a half smile starting to form. "Don't you think they would try to get me the way they got Capone?"

"I imagine your financial lawyers are as good as theirs."

"Yes, they have to be." He was baiting me now, trying to see if I would lead him into anything new.

I pushed out of the chair. "Well, Don Ponti, I don't give a rat's tail what the IRS does to you. All I want is the guy who killed Dooley. This time it isn't just me. Captain Chambers is part of this package and he's got the NYPD behind him, and that's one big load of professionalism to buck up against."

"Somehow I think you have a person in mind," Ponti said.

I started toward the door, then turned and said, "I'd

keep a close watch on your boy Ugo. He hasn't got the expertise we old-timers have."

Ponti nodded again, but the frown had creased his forehead, too, and I knew his brain was doing mental gymnastics trying to put different meaning to my words.

Nobody was at the door when I went down. I stood there a minute, then went to the curb and waited. Two blocks down headlights flashed on and the cabby I had instructed to wait drove up, let me in and took off for my apartment. When I got out I tipped him again, got a big grin from him and went inside.

There was a message on my answering machine and I touched the button. It was Velda and she wanted me to call her. The short meet with Ponti had wiped me out and I hoped she wasn't going to get heavy on me. For a brief second I wondered if I would miss the single life at all. I had gotten pretty good at doing everything solo and taking on a partner might entail things I didn't expect. I was hoping she could make biscuits.

But Velda was a smart doll. She laughed when I said, "I'm alive."

"So what else is new?"

"What's the message?"

"I can answer the office phone from my apartment here," she said. "It helped while you were doing R and R in Florida."

"Who called?"

"An old movie star named Ralph Morgan."

"That Ralph Morgan is deceased, kitten."

"This one wasn't. He said he'd see you tomorrow. Be at the Waldorf at eleven."

"Good," I told her. "We'll both go. I'll pick you up for breakfast at eight."

"I could come over there and make it for you," she suggested. Her tone was very silky.

"No," I said.

"Why not?"

"Because if I have to hurt, you have to ache a little too. Just keep your knickers on."

She laughed again as she hung up.

IT DIDN'T SEEM POSSIBLE, but the man in the light grey suit was the doctor, all right. It was his face, nicely tanned and cleanly shaved with a styled haircut that gave him a professional touch only old doctors could wear properly. The suit was new and expensive and evidently tailor made.

"You clean up real good," I said.

"There was more money in my account than I expected."

"How's the car?"

"A real dreamboat, like we used to say."

"No trouble?"

He shook his head. "You were right about everything. All the paperwork is in order and nobody said a word about the past. I think Florida is a good place for doctors."

"Well, they have a lot of prospective patients in the retiree group."

"How have you been feeling?"

"It's been exciting, but I'm not hustling any. Nobody's punched me in the ribs or tried to kill me."

"You know," he said with a clinical touch in his voice, "you shouldn't even be getting stressed out, Mike."

"Now you tell me."

"Coming back here may kill you, my friend. That wouldn't make me very happy at all."

From the corner of the room Velda said, "Me either."

"I'm referring to you as well as some of the other company he keeps, young lady," Dr. Morgan said to her. "There are times when tender loving care can get out of hand."

"It beats getting blown up," she snapped back.

"What?"

"Someone doped up the engine of his car. One turn of the key and we would have been history," she added.

He glanced at me for confirmation and I nodded. "The key didn't get turned, doc—we're still here."

His eyes narrowed somewhat. "Did it have to do with this . . . Ponti affair?"

"I don't think it was the old man."

"Ugo, then?"

"How'd you know about him?"

"I researched everything I could on the incident. I even went into some of the events of the past. As a matter of fact, I have even met some of the don's associates in the Metro Health Club I belong to."

"What kind of club was that?"

"Mainly doctors and lawyers who got light exercise and a lot of talk when they got fed up with business. The lawyers had some of their clients along on occasions and we were introduced."

"Remember any of them?"

"It wouldn't matter," he said. "They're all dead now.

They were powerhouses in their businesses, but every one was pretty old. Harris was probably the youngest and he was crowding eighty when he got killed."

It was Velda who asked it. "Harris who?"

"Oh, they called him something like bad back."

"Could it have been Slipped Disk?"

Morgan's eyebrows rose in a gesture of approval. "Right you are, young lady. That is what they called him. He never seemed to mind, though."

"What did you know about him?" Velda persisted.

"He had money, that was for sure. A little rough around the edges, but I guess you'd have to be when you're selling *liquor* in New York." He looked over at me. "You know this man?"

"I only know about him, doc. What can you tell me?"

"He had mighty good booze, all Canadian, that's for sure. He was able to sell it at incredibly low prices to select places in the city. Everybody figured he had a hijacking operation going, but there was no report of anything being stolen."

"How long did he operate?"

"That I don't know, but he called it quits about six months before he died."

"You know, for a doctor you kept some strange company too," I said.

"Doctors never meet normal people. Everybody's always sick."

"Harris too?"

"No, not him. He had a rugged look, tanned up, broken nose, that sort of thing. He even dressed like a country boy. When I met him he had on a plaid woolen shirt and corduroy pants. It didn't seem to matter, though. He had as much money as anybody else."

"He pretty friendly with Ponti?"

"Beats me, Mike. I kind of got the idea that it was Ponti who introduced him around. Just something I heard." He squinted at me and added, "Why?"

"Because Slipped Disk Harris buddied up with my old friend who got himself killed."

"What was wrong with that?"

"It was an unlikely combination. Marcos Dooley didn't have hoods for pals."

"Mike . . . there was a time when a real bootlegger wasn't a hood. He could be nothing more than a friendly neighborhood distributor of an item the federal government took away from you."

I grinned at him. Coming from an old rummy, it was nicely put.

Velda was leaning forward on her seat now. There was a set to her face that meant that something was clicking in her mind. All I had to do was stare at her and she said, "Suppose I probe around a little, Mike."

"Be careful."

"Look who's talking. Will you be at the office?"

"Probably. If I'm not, leave a message."

She told us both so long and left.

When the door shut, Morgan said, "Take off your shirt, Mike."

"Come on, doc, I'm okay. All I need are the pills."

"You know better than that. Let me take a look at you."

I didn't argue. I did as I was told, stripped down and let him poke all around the ugly sore spot that was still inflamed and grisly looking. He did what he had to do and bandaged the wound. From the sounds he was making I knew things weren't as good as they could have been.

"You should have stayed in Florida, Mike."

"No choice, doc."

"You can choose to die too. I told you . . . absolute rest

is vital. You're right back in the kind of mess that can do you in for good."

"Pal," I said, "your bedside manner is still lousy."

"So's your attitude."

"I'm taking it easy. I told you that."

"The hell you are. That wound is starting to open again. Antibiotics can take it down, but you're going to have to make up your own mind what you're going to do. If you were back in the army you'd be hospitalized and strapped down to a bed. As for me, all I can do is give you advice that you don't want to take."

"Is it that bad?"

He made a face. He didn't have to tell me the rest. Finally he said, "If you really want to marry that girl, you'd better think hard on what I'm telling you." From his pocket he took out a pad of prescription blanks, wrote on two of them and held them out. At least I could read his writing. "That's in case you run out of these." He gave me two vials, both containing my usual medication.

"Suppose something *does* happen, doc . . . if that thing gets ripped open or somebody really creams me?"

"You have your famous .45 with you?"

"Handy enough."

"Save the last bullet for yourself."

"Boy," I told him, "you're about as consoling as a mongoose is to a cobra."

I wasn't in my office more than a minute when Pat called me from his car phone. He was on the way uptown and his voice sounded tight when he said it was imperative that we talk. While I waited for him I sketched out a few notes in outline form to keep all the details in order and when I finished page four I heard the front door open.

Pat walked in, his mouth grim, but it was the man with him that got me a little edgy. I nodded to Pat and said to Homer Watson, "Well, good to see you again." I waved to the chairs and they both sat down. Neither one of them was holding paperwork, so I asked, "You recording this interview?"

Watson smiled gently and patted his pocket.

I opened my desk drawer and took out my miniature Sony, put it in front of me, touched the *on* button, gave the date and occasion and asked them, "Then you don't mind if I do?" Neither one answered.

Finally Pat said, "Do you know what you're into, Mike?"

"Unless somebody tells me, I'm running blank. But let's cut to the chase. You and Homer here are scratching for something and you have me right in the dirt. Somehow all this seems to center around Marcos Dooley, and I wasn't there when he was shot. I came back to New York to pay my last respects before he died because we had been in the same war together."

"And you two had a big talk together before he went," Pat reminded me.

"Right. It was at your instigation, pal, so what's the beef?"

"The gist of your conversation," Homer said quietly.

"We went through all this before."

"No, we only touched on the edges."

I held up my hand and stopped him. "You know, back in the eighties when all of the agencies were pushing the RICO statute to hit the Mafia, you got bugs into the private and protected home of Paul Castellano, you bugged Tony Corallo's Jaguar, you had super-scopes and parabolic microphones to keep everybody under surveillance and you couldn't even cover one shot-up war veteran in a city hospital? Come on, what do I look like, a spy of spies?"

"You look like somebody who stumbled into something accidentally."

"And you want to know what it is?"

There was a short pause, and Watson said, "That's right."

"Quid pro quo," I told him. "You tell me."

His nod was imperceptible, but it was there. "There seems to be some soul-searching among the families in the mob. There are several high-ranking firms of attorneys and financial houses investigating illegal activities."

I grinned at him and said, "And they can't find out where the money went."

Curtly, he said, "No." I waited a moment and he added, "It started disappearing about 1986, it seems."

"That's not very definite."

"Our inside sources couldn't do any better." I was about to say something, but he anticipated it with a smile. "They sent me. It seems that my superiors think I have a terrier mentality with an uncanny smell for money."

"So?"

"Ever since Cotti went down the tubes there's been a scramble for succession. Not only for his former position, but for a clamp on the entire organization. The new blood is different. It's smarter, it has different ideals. It seems they were pretty well put out when they found the money coffers empty."

"Where do I come in, Homer. Or Dooley?"

"Your friend left a trail of sorts. Lorenzo Ponti did a lot of talking with him in private, seemingly about nothing. On many occasions there were other bosses on hand who took the same attitude toward Dooley that Ponti did."

"Dooley wasn't in the mob," I ground out. "You ought to know that."

"I do. What I can't figure out is, *what was he?*"

"He was a caretaker, for Pete's sake. He was a paid employee. He was a nothing. Damn, you guys did a background check on him, didn't you?"

"Yes."

"What did you come up with?"

"Nothing." He leaned forward, his hands on his knees. "The government estimates that over the past not too many years, many billions of dollars have been siphoned from the economy into the hands of those who control the Mafia. At best, the recipients could only have spent a fraction of it, but somehow it's all disappeared. We've had agents on it a long time checking out all the normal depositing facilities, we've had cooperation from police agencies and financial institutions, but we find nothing."

"And you're out in the field all by yourself?"

"No, but I'm the one concerned with you."

"How did you tie up with Pat here?"

"Because he had an interest in Dooley too. Then you came into it."

"Homer," I asked him, "were you ever in the military?"

"No."

"You can form some pretty tight friendships under combat conditions."

"So I understand."

"Dooley, Pat and I were a team. If Dooley had walked off with Fort Knox it wouldn't be important enough to worry about when he was dying. Even if I owned the place I could have forgiven him. We were buddies, see?"

He stared at me a few moments, then nodded slowly. "Where do you go from here?"

"I want to find out who killed him."

Homer Watson got up slowly. His hand dipped into his pocket to shut off his miniature tape recorder. He waved a finger at Pat and walked to the door. With his hand on the knob, he turned around, looked at me and asked, "Then what, Mr. Hammer?"

I let him see all my teeth in a big grin.

When the door shut behind him, Pat's face relaxed. "With eighty billion you probably could buy Ford and GM together."

"You have a good memory, Pat."

"If it weren't for Watson I would have thought you were making it all up. But I did a rundown on him. He got our association from newspaper clips. I got his through police sources. He's a very competent investigator. Not tough, just able."

"Then I guess I'll have a tail on me from now on."

"You guess correctly, pal."

"NYPD involved?"

"Nobody has entered a complaint so far."

"How about our lady assistant DA?"

"So far she's been pretty quiet. But she can be pretty sneaky too," he reminded me.

"Okay, where do you stand, old buddy?"

Pat let out a little laugh that sounded more like a cough. "I'm going to watch you work, Mike. This case is over the death of a nobody for billions of dollars that are unrecorded and possibly do not exist and you trying to kill yourself when nobody is around to pay you."

"You sound a little unconvinced."

"Then convince me."

"Would a hot pastrami sandwich and a cold beer do it? I'll have coffee with mine."

* * *

Velda didn't get to my apartment until eight o'clock. Whatever she had done, her shoes were scuffed up and she was shiny with sweat. She didn't say hello, she simply threw her purse down on a chair and stated, "I have to take a shower."

You don't question beautiful women in that condition. I pointed toward the bathroom and went to my closet to get her the terrycloth robe she had bought for me. I heard her turn the water on and the shower door slide closed and all I could think about was how the hell I was going to get out of a compromising situation like this. Here we were, un-ringed, but vocally engaged, and she was going to get me all wrapped up like a spider does a trapped fly and I'd forget all my no-sex-until-after-marriage attitudes.

Downstairs there was a dry cleaner who kept odd hours and I picked up the phone and got his cigarette-husky hello. He said he could do a quick dry clean job for me in an hour and would send a kid right up for the clothes. In less than five minutes I had passed the garments out, then sat down and watched the TV news. Girls love to take long showers. When they're real dirty they take longer ones. I watched a local show and the first twenty minutes of *Discovery*, got the clothes back from the kid and was having a cup of coffee when I heard the water cut off. When the shower door opened I gave her a couple of minutes to dry off, then walked over, opened the door and handed in the robe. I heard her quiet "Damn!" and she pulled the door shut. I knew what she was going to do. She was going to come out in nothing but a cleverly draped bath towel that could fall off whenever she wanted it to.

"Wiseguy," she said when she came out.

I pointed to her clothes neatly hung over the back of

the sofa. Velda knew what I had done. "Smart-ass," she told me, but she was smiling. "I still have to get dressed."

"I'll go in the kitchen when you're ready," I said.

"Are you always going to be like this?"

"Only until after we're married. Remember, you started all this."

"Mike," she told me sweetly, "I think this is going to be fun." She picked up her purse and sat in the chair, doing that bit with a crossing of the legs that women are so good at. With the fingers of one hand she spread apart the terry-cloth collar at her throat, her tongue deliberately wetting her lips.

"What have you got for me?" I asked her.

She gave me a silent smile for a moment, then: "I called in a couple of favors and ran your phone bill up, but got some interesting information. That estate Ponti has up in the Adirondacks is in his wife's name, free and clear with all taxes paid. It's worth about two hundred thousand, the property being scenic, but not good for cultivation. It's on the side of a mountain with a slate base and probably not a good site for development. The house is nice, but modest."

I stared at her face and said, "Now surprise me."

"Harris and Ponti seemed to be buddies of some sort, so I had surrounding properties checked out. Nothing bordered on Ponti's estate, but Harris had his own place on the side of another mountain area about five miles away. Nothing fancy here . . . just a big old log cabin put up in the twenties, an open-fronted shed and a three-wagon barn."

"No outhouse?"

"It has indoor plumbing."

"Who lives there?"

"Some old guy. He could be a caretaker. The place belongs to Harris' daughter who lives in the village."

"If it has a caretaker, the place must make some kind of money."

"My source said slate was mined there at times. As a matter of fact, it seems to be a revived industry since the Japanese have taken most of the product. There's another major area in Granville, not too far away."

"One last thing. Who was your source?"

"An old admirer who works for the state of New York. I met him at a party. No, we never kissed. No, we never even held hands."

"Way to go," I told her jokingly.

She blew me a kiss. "Where are we now?"

I reached over, turned the TV off and sat back. "Let's see what we have. One killing and a big stink. Dooley was an innocuous figure, so his murder couldn't have been over any direct involvement with the big stink. Now, that stink has been in the making for some time. You don't run off with billions overnight. A lot of thought went into that scheme. It was started when the dons were alive, when the Mafia had a different sort of organizational setup. But now, except for Lorenzo Ponti, there are new heads of the families. They're younger and smarter, but the feds and the new laws are harder to deal with and the money, the big power, isn't there anymore and the families are hurting."

"Where could it go, Mike?"

"It hasn't been destroyed, kitten."

"And it hasn't been spent."

"But it's been stolen."

"Supposing it *was* stolen. Who is big enough to steal it?"

"The government could," I said.

"Which government?"

I took another sip of my coffee. It had grown cold and tasted terrible. "It would have to be pretty damn powerful and mighty devious. To make a move like that it would have to have a need so big it would take a chance of being obliterated if it were caught."

Velda sat there, her fingertips touching her lips. "What are you thinking, Mike?"

"They were caught, but after the heist was over. They died for it because the killers weren't sure about things."

"Why is Ponti still alive?"

"That don is smarter. They have to keep someone alive to set them on the right track and he'll stay breathing until the loot is recovered."

"Then he'll be killed?"

"Most likely. His kid Ugo is a trigger-happy slob who wouldn't think twice about rubbing out the old man if he could inherit the cash. In fact, he could have explored this situation and figured out where Dooley stood and arranged to have his father killed in a staged gang war. That didn't work, so he took Dooley out before the guy could decide to open up to the authorities."

"Where did Dooley stand?"

"Between a rock and a hard place. He was a person who could do a job, but not somebody who would be sorely missed if he had a fatal accident." The jarring ring of the phone cut in, making us both jump.

"Who knows you're here?" Velda asked.

I shook my head and picked up the receiver. An odd voice said, "Mr. Hammer?" I said that it was. "This is Marshall Brotorrio, Mr. Hammer."

Then I remembered him. He was in charge of the repository where I had placed Dooley's remains.

"Sorry to be calling you so late."

"No trouble. What's up?"

"My night man was making his usual rounds when he found the urn you had placed here taken from the niche and emptied on the floor. Whoever did it kicked the casing across the aisle, putting a big dent in it."

"What about the ashes?"

"Those were scattered, as if someone had kicked them too."

"Any sign of a break-in?"

"Oh, yes. One window was out. The glass was broken, the catch opened and the window pushed back. There was no difficulty there at all. It must have happened right after my man came on. He was eating supper on the other side of the building and never heard a thing."

"Have you called the police?"

"No, not yet. This is such a personal matter . . . nothing else has been touched . . . that I thought you should know about it first. What do you suggest?"

"Tell you what, Marshall, why don't you sweep the remains back into the urn and put it back where it belongs."

"There could be floor dirt and . . ."

"Dooley won't care about that."

"Should I call the police?"

"That'll only get you bad publicity. You wouldn't want your clients thinking vandals could get to the remains of their loved ones, would you?"

"Certainly not!"

"Then just get the window fixed, Marshall, and we'll forget about it."

Velda was waiting intently and I told her what had happened. She said, "Somebody thought you hid something in that urn."

"They sure got teed off when they found it empty."

"Who knew where you put the ashes?"

"Marvin Dooley knew, but it's unlikely he'd figure I'd

stash anything out there. No, it was somebody who knew the score. I'd finger Ugo for that deal. He was at the funeral parlor and he could have seen Richmond take me aside and talk to me. He might not have followed me himself, but someone else in his crowd could have."

"You think he made the break-in himself?"

"Let's consider that a distinct possibility. The bad news is that since he didn't find anything he'll keep looking."

"Mike . . ." she started.

"What?"

"Did you open the urn at all?"

"No, why?"

"Maybe he did find something and kicked the empty jar around as a red herring."

I let it run through my mind, then said, "Think happy thoughts, will you?"

"Boss, I'm not Peter Pan." She grinned and stood up, letting the terrycloth robe swirl around her. It was really something, seeing her like that. My mind kept telling me that one day it would all be mine, that tall loveliness of a sweet-smelling woman. All I had to do was stay alive. "Now, what are you going to do with me?"

"You have two choices, doll. I'm going to let that hole in me get a nice, soft rest in my bed. So . . . you can either get dressed and go home, or sack it in on the couch. Alone."

"You're really trying to ruin your reputation, aren't you." She made a definite statement out of that, but her smile took the edge off.

7

IN THE MORNING I filled the coffee pot, pushed the ON button and got dressed while Velda still made soft sleep sounds on the couch. I brushed my teeth, shaved and had a quick cup of fresh ground Dunkin' Donuts special blend, wrote a note and left it on the coffee table where she'd be sure to spot it.

Outside, the morning didn't seem too encouraging, so I slipped into my trenchcoat and went down to the lobby. Bill Raabe was still on security detail and waved me over to his cubbyhole where he was sorting out packages.

I told him good morning and he said, "Mike, you got anything going on?"

"Like what, Billy?"

"You know, trouble."

"Why do you ask?"

"Two cars have been keeping a watch on this place ever since I came on at midnight."

"Cops?"

"No way. Both are Buick sedans. The unmarked police cars aren't that rich. There were a couple of guys in each car."

"Recognize them?"

"Couldn't get a good look at them. A couple of times one would park across the street fifteen or twenty minutes. I could see a cigarette glow inside, so they were there."

He gave me a quick grin. "I did spot the first three numbers on one buggy. They were 411."

"That'll help," I told him.

"Suppose they were stolen?"

"Then it won't help at all," I said.

"Maybe you'll get lucky."

I looked at my watch. It was two minutes past seven. "When did they go by last?"

"Just before you came down. Look, you can go down the basement and out the back way. Jackie is loading up the air freight truck and he can get you out of the area."

"Good idea, pal."

"By the way," he added, "your secretary told me about somebody trying to take you out with a car bomb. We've installed some new spotting equipment down there."

"You know, I'm going to lose my lease yet," I said.

Bill called Jackie on the interphone and after I helped him carry out a couple of packages, he carried me down to Third Avenue where I got out and waited. Nobody was tailing me at all. A taxi spotted me on the corner, swerved in and stopped.

Just in time. It started to rain. It was too early for the sky to be dirty, so you could see through the big drops that kissed the windows.

A block away from the precinct house was a corner restaurant that had been in the same family since the turn of the century. It was a bar and grill where the food was the greatest if you weren't into French cuisine. At the end of each shift the bar crowd would have a couple of quickies before getting on the subway, but the steady customers were the old-timers, the retirees who couldn't get away from *the Job.* Ninety percent were either divorced or widowed. They were grey and wrinkled, but there was no denying what they had been before retirement age had swept them into the inactive ranks.

It had been a long time since I had seen Peppy Marlow. He wore a derby then and an overcoat with a velvet collar. He was a three-gun cop with two pieces on his hip and a throwaway in an ankle holster. The young cops used to call him *cowboy,* but never to his face. He was head of the squad that tried to enforce prohibition and stayed with vice until he retired.

I wondered if he'd remember me, but I shouldn't have bothered. He grinned up from his coffee cup, and said, "Well, Mike Hammer, the old shooter himself."

"Hi, Sarge."

"Come on, Mike. Let's not embarrass the rookies. I'm still Peppy. Gettin' old, but still Peppy. Sit down."

I slipped the trenchcoat off, draped it over an empty chair and sat down.

"You eat yet, Mike?"

"I had coffee."

"Try the Mexican eggs. Something new they came up with."

A chubby waitress with a big smile suddenly stood over me. "How about some bran flakes and two percent milk?" She looked a little surprised, but took my order.

"What's that all about, Mike?"

"Doctor's orders. I'm on a damn diet. I got shot up pretty bad."

His "oh" meant so what else is new, but he understood completely.

For a few minutes we talked over the old days, then when our orders came, Peppy said, "Let's see, the last time we made contact was about twelve years ago. You wanted something then and I suppose you want something now."

I tasted the coffee, spooned up some bran flakes and said, "You have a good memory for the old prohibition days?"

"Why, you gonna write my biography?"

"I wouldn't think of it. You got any dope on Slipped Disk Harris?"

"Sure. He's been dead a long time."

"How about when he was alive?"

"Slippery weasel, that one. A nice guy, but a real careful operator." He took a forkful of eggs. "Whatta you want to know?"

"His operation. How did he work it?"

Peppy shrugged, gathering his thoughts together. "He worked the high-class stuff. When the slobs were paying big prices for watered-down booze he was delivering the best Canadian you could buy. It cost, but it was top quality."

"Where did he get it?"

"The trucks came down from Canada and he rode in front of the convoy in an old Reo. In those days the roadways were different and he had his routes mapped out all the way. A real sharp character, that guy. He was only hijacked twice, and those jobs were small potatoes on light loads."

"How about the feds?" I asked him.

"Hell, he drove those guys nutty. They never even came near him. They knew what he was carrying and thought they knew his routes, but their roadblocks never turned up a damn thing."

"Didn't he have a transfer spot?"

"He must have," Peppy told me. "He couldn't take the trucks into the city. Someplace he off-loaded to autos to make the final delivery. Never once was he intercepted."

"Old Harris must have made a bundle."

"You'd better believe it. And you know something? None of us ever figured out how he worked it, but we were glad he did. The idiots who passed the Volstead Act had their heads up their tails when they tried to play moral good guys. All they did was invite the hoods into the action."

"Yeah, but long after prohibition he went back to work supplying the good stuff to joints all over the city. Nobody could figure that deal out at all."

"Mike, you know what was strange about that?"

"What?"

"With all the tight government control on booze, from distilling to sales, not one brand maker showed any phony paperwork. They had no theft reports that weren't minor and not ever a hint of any conspiracy. When Harris died, all the action stopped. Nobody even tried to step into his shoes."

For a couple of minutes we both sat there without talking. When the waitress filled my coffee cup again I said, "What do you think, Peppy?"

"I'm not. I'm just wondering what you're doing back in the old bootleg days?"

"You remember Marcos Dooley, Peppy?"

"Yeah. He just got killed."

"Someplace he's involved in this."

"Baloney. He was like you, too young to be in that mess."

"Then what about Lorenzo Ponti?"

Peppy nodded and grinned. "Now he was into the bootleg business. That was where he got his start. He's still up there in the family circle, though I hear the young turks are easing him out little by little. You'd think those old Mafia families would have been wiped out by now, but they're still in there. Smoother, better educated with higher priced lawyers, but still there."

"What do you hear that's special, Peppy?"

"I hear lots, Mike, but I'm not going to jeopardize what they're doing on the job. You know that."

"No sweat. Just one thing more. Where do you think Harris was off-loading his booze trucks?"

"Someplace upstate," he said. "He didn't work the coastline stuff at all. All his loads came out of Canada by truck." He paused, then continued, "Let me tell you what one of the fed guys thought. They were always looking for a convoy, but the trucks came out singly, not drawing much attention, and followed a course until they converged. Then Harris picked them up in his Reo and led them to the area where they unloaded."

That made sense, all right. I finished my coffee and picked up both the checks. Just as I thanked Peppy for the information a pair of old cronies came in and sat down with him. They had the same look that he had, and idly I wondered if they were still playing cops. It was a hard routine to get out of your system.

It was Pat's day off and I met him outside his apartment building. He greeted me with, "Has the DA's office reached you yet?"

I shook my head. "Why would they?"

"Because somebody reported Dooley's ashes being

kicked all over that place you put them. You know about that?"

"Sure."

He gave me that disgusted look again. "Why didn't you say something?"

"Like what? Marshall Brotorrio called me to tell me what happened. I told him to put the dust back and forget it. Who called it in?"

"Apparently the security man who discovered it."

"Then where does the DA come in?"

"Dooley's death is still under investigation and for some reason Florence Lake has a big interest in it."

"Like about eighty-nine billion bucks' worth, Pat?" My tone had a flat seriousness to it.

He turned his head slowly and gave me a penetrating glance. "You were serious about that, weren't you?"

I nodded. "Who corroborated it, Pat?"

"Officially, nobody." When I didn't say anything he added, "Homer Watson mentioned some astronomical number like that in passing."

"In passing, my behind," I said.

"Okay, he was feeling me out, but there was nothing I could tell him. I had forgotten your strange line of thinking about the cartons."

I grinned at him, then let out a little laugh. "No, you didn't, Pat. You just stored it away. Hell, you never forget anything."

"A guy can sure buy a big car with that kind of dough," Pat said quietly. "You going to tell me what it's all about?"

A cab came by and I flagged it down. When we got in I gave the driver the address in Brooklyn and settled into the seat. "I wish I knew, Pat. Maybe we can find something in Dooley's pad."

We didn't have to kick in any doors to get in. I rang the

bell and Marvin Dooley opened the door for us. "You didn't take long to move in," I told him.

"No problem," he said. "I got a good lawyer." He looked at Pat, his eyes picking him right up as being a cop. "What're you guys doing here?"

"We want to look through the house, that's what."

"Supposing I don't want to let you."

"If you want a rap in the mouth it's okay with me," I told him.

He thought for a moment, then held the door open. "Aw, come on in. There's nothing in here to find anyway. I already tore the place apart, what was left of it."

"Oh?"

"Somebody else was already here. Hell, he tore out some of the walls, ripped up the furniture and the mattresses . . . man, what a mess this was."

It only took a quick tour to see what he was talking about. The search had been detailed and thorough, but it was an amateur job. Pat said, "He wasn't squeezed for time, that's for sure." The marks of a rough tool scarred the woodwork where boards had been pried loose and a sharp blade had been used to get into any stuffed material.

When we finished the inspection Pat asked, "What do *you* see, Mike?"

"He never found anything, that's what I see. He never stopped looking."

"Yeah. And he was neat about it. At least he didn't make any noise. Nothing was thrown over. It was picked up, turned over carefully and checked out. If anything had been found the search would have ended right there."

I agreed and we both went back to the living room, where Marvin was straightening up the remnants of the sofa. "Junk," he said, "it's all junk now." He looked at us, his eyes darting back and forth between Pat and me.

"When did you get here?" I asked him.

"About an hour ago." When I didn't answer him, he said, "I was figuring on moving in. I told you I was going to. Hell, I own it now."

"I don't think you'll be very comfortable," Pat said. "You speak to anybody outside?"

Marvin nodded vigorously. "Damn well told. Except for a kid across the street nobody saw nothing! At least the kid remembered some man who stopped by twice and when he didn't get an answer he left. He came back a little later, stood there a minute, then came on in. The kid said he thought somebody had opened the door for him. Hell, that old lock wouldn't've kept a cat out. He jimmied that door open."

"The kid describe him?"

"Nah. He was only a strange guy to the kid." He stopped and wiped his face. "His old lady was at the window, though. She knew who it was."

Evidently Marvin was expecting a big reaction from us, but when he didn't get it, he said, "He had been here a few times before. Drove up then. Big car, brand new." We still just looked at him and waited. "Twice he got in the guy's car and drove off. The old lady thought my old man worked for him."

Not him, I thought. *Dooley had worked for his father. It was Ugo who had tossed Dooley's place looking for any line to unravel the puzzle.*

Marvin seemed disappointed when we told him thanks and so long. Outside we walked toward the corner in silence, then I told Pat, "Ugo is shaking loose, pal. He hit the urn and Dooley's own house and hasn't found anything yet."

"I was just thinking that. You know what's coming next, don't you?"

"Certainly. He'll be coming after me."

"What're your plans, kiddo?"

"I want to meet him in my own backyard. He'll only think he's setting the stage."

"And I suppose you'll want backup on this?"

"Come on, I'm a citizen. I'd expect it." I saw the frown start on his face and knew what was bothering him. "You can forget it, if you want to, Pat."

"No, I can't forget it. I was close to Dooley too. What bothers me is any personal involvement that might screw up the works. Dooley wasn't a big enough event to get his killing on the front page, but if you're really onto the right kind of money numbers, this fracas has got the makings of one big bust."

"Then stay out of it."

"Mike . . . you know I can't. Not now. You made it more than just a killing. Dooley opened up a can of worms and you took the bait." His eyes tightened somewhat. "Now, so did I."

"You want to make it official business?"

"I can see them trying to get a word out of you," he said. "There's not a damn thing they can charge you with and you're not about to give anything away, are you?"

"Dooley dropped it in my lap, Pat, remember? The conversation wasn't recorded and all he did was hand me a joker out of the deck and tell me to make a royal flush of it."

At the corner Pat stopped and stared down the avenue for a cab. "You'll be tangling with the feds and the DA's office, for starters, Mike. They're both heavy hitters with big teams to cover all the bases. You know what you're up against?"

"You always ask me that, Pat. The answer is the same. No, I don't know, but I expect I'll find out pretty soon, don't you?"

He grunted and waved his hand toward a cab. "At least you got that right."

When the cab stopped we both got in and Pat gave the driver his midtown address. I told him to let me off at Thirty-fourth Street and we stayed quiet until I got out. When the cab pulled away I grabbed another and went up to Bud Langston's office, where his first words were, "That was a short week, Mike."

"This could be a friendly visit," I said.

"But it's not, right?"

"Right. Things are beginning to happen."

"And you want body armor to protect your worn old frame, I imagine."

"What I want is to see this stuff. If it's for real it puts another light on what I'm doing."

"Oh, it's real, all right. And this time everything was going for us. Coulter and I had a locker together at the club where we used to try out our gadgets in the pool. He mentioned a package he had left there with that new material in it."

"And?"

Bud got up and walked to the closet and came back with what looked like a long-sleeved black sweatshirt draped over a wire coat hanger. "You still an extra large?"

"You guessed right."

He held out the hanger and I took the gadget off the wire. For a few seconds I let my fingers run over the fabric itself, noticing the satin-like texture. It was full-waist length, yet couldn't have weighed more than a few ounces. "And this will stop a bullet?"

"I told you . . . anything under a twenty-millimeter."

"That's hard to believe."

"Believe it, Mike. I've seen the tests carried out."

"How does it work?"

Bud gave me a sad look, and said, "Why is a single strand of spiderweb stronger than a steel wire of the same dimensions?"

"Beats me," I told him.

"Then stop asking silly questions. I fused the material into something you can wear. The trouble with a lot of armor is it leaves the arms open to bullet wounds. This thing is like wearing an undershirt. There's a flap that comes up between your legs that you fasten with Velcro. Pretty neat, eh?"

"I didn't know you could sew," I said. "You want it back?"

His eyes seemed to cloud up a little. He had known me too long. "When you're done with it, Mike."

I nodded, told him thanks and went out and got a cab back to my office.

The rain had started again. This time it had picked up sky dirt and smelled funny. The drops were smaller than before, nature having a last laugh before deciding to drench the city with a downpour. I was glad I had my trenchcoat with me. The belt had started to bite into my side and I loosened it. It was a half hour late for the pain pills, so I just sat back and made faces until I got to the office.

Velda said I looked pretty pasty when I walked in. I felt even worse until the pills took hold. My legs were shaky and my head was light. I knew I was breathing, but couldn't seem to feel like anything was going into my lungs. I swung around in my desk chair and leaned back, my feet going up to the windowsill. She had seen me do that so often she figured I was all right, but I was far from it. The greyness of the day outside the glass panes got darker than it should have and I felt as if I were going off into deep sleep in a black alley that was dark and empty.

My head didn't snap up. The motion was very slow and deliberate. The color outside the window came back and I could feel myself breathing again. I kept thinking that living was a real pleasure and anything that had to be done to prolong it should be done.

When Velda came back she was holding the body armor shirt. "What is this, Mike?"

I didn't feel like going into long explanations. "Something scuba divers use underwater."

"What do you want it for?"

"Sunken treasure, doll," I said.

"You?"

"Let me have my dreams, will you?"

She tossed it on my desk. "You *really* need a wife, Mikey boy."

"Sure I do," I agreed with a grunt. "Now sit down in the client's chair. I need a sounding board. It's not like the old days anymore. I have a head full of details, but I can't seem to get them lined up. Azi's .357 got me in the side, but it's messed up my thinking."

With a look of understanding, Velda sat down. She didn't have to take notes. She was one of those people who had that ability to remember an entire lecture on criminology almost verbatim and repeat it back afterward. It was something she did when she wanted to, but not bothering otherwise. Even the way she sat was part of her deliberate intention to absorb every word I said and the tilt of her head reminded me of a feral cat waiting outside a mouse hole.

So I gave her all the elements of the case as I knew them, and when I was done, went over them again with suppositions thrown in to bolster theory. When I was done I felt like having a cold beer, but the ache in my side said no.

"What do you think, kitten?"

"You're the detective," she reminded me.

"Unless you forgot to renew it, you have a ticket too."

"Wouldn't you do better asking Pat?"

"If Dooley had wanted that he would have asked Pat himself. This is something he dumped on me. Sooner or later Pat is going to have to come in on it, but right now his job is running down Dooley's killer. Everybody else is playing a big guessing game and they have the board nailed to my back. They hate me for not holding still long enough to let the darts hit it."

"It's all about money, isn't it, Mike?"

"Eighty-nine billion dollars worth. It sounds almost indecent to say it."

"And nobody is sure of where it is."

"Hell, nobody can prove it even was. If the story is true, the old dons got screwed out of it, but they're all dead except for Ponti. The young guys in the mob have a good idea that it's somewhere . . . but can't locate it. What's funny is that it isn't like looking for a needle in a haystack at all. It would be one huge pile of cartons packed tight with cash or negotiables . . . and nobody wants to talk about it at all."

"Mike . . . how did the feds come in on this?"

"They're money mice, doll. They can smell the stuff and will follow the trail until they die. They don't care how they clip the public, but don't let anybody hold out a dollar on them. Look at how they got Capone."

She considered that a minute, then smiled gently. "Modern technology. In Capone's day they had comptometers, today we have computers. They're going to run that money down with electronics. The new dons used them to shake out the possibility of a hoard and we don't even have a laptop."

"We don't need one," I said. "Electronics didn't squirrel that much cash away. It was being collected and hidden before the computer age hit us."

She was thinking the same thing I was, and it showed in the way she pursed her lips. "We still follow the money trail, don't we?"

"Right you are, doll, but before we do, let's verify those big numbers. *Time, Newsweek, U.S. News and World Report* . . . all those magazines have covered the actions of the families. Go hire some researchers to get the details. Pick up what you can from the newspapers and don't sweat out specifics. Anything they got would have been an estimated figure anyway. We know what the drug revenue is figured at, so put it all together in big round numbers and see what we get. And by the way, have we got enough money to pay for researchers?"

"*That* much we have," Velda reassured me.

"Let's do it then."

Ever since the army days I had never stayed in the sack after six. The coffee was made, my face was shaved and I was all dressed when the authoritative knock came on my door. I could have told who it was. Unless a badge was flashed on Bill Raabe and he was told officially not to announce the visitors he wouldn't have let the president in. But here was Mr. Authority with a big fist who looked startled as hell when I jerked the door open and said, "Well, Miss Lake and Mr. Watson, you're just in time for coffee." I looked at my watch. "You city people sure get up late. Where have you been?"

Florence Lake smiled feebly. Homer harrumphed and

let me shut the door behind him. I ushered them into the living room, then went back and got two cups of freshly brewed Dunkin' Donuts coffee for them. They both muttered thanks, but I had sure put a big dent in their surprise visit. Some people can be all shook up by an official call that early in the morning.

So I let them sit. Finally Florence Lake said, "We have done an exhaustive study of Mr. Dooley's past. A lot of man-hours went into this and we came up with some interesting details."

"Good for you," I told her. "You sharing this information?"

"We may."

I took a taste of my coffee and set the cup down. "Look, Miss Lake, I don't give a hoot one way or another what you tell me. If it's something I wanted to know I'd find it out myself. Let's not play games. What have you got?"

The two of them exchanged glances, then she pulled a few papers from her pocket and laid them on the coffee table. They were receipt forms, six from Gerrity Trucking company, listing week-long rentals each time and four separate orders from Watertight Carton Company. The dates were years old.

I looked them over, shrugged, and said, "What's this suppose to mean?"

"Your friend rented those trucks and bought those cartons in his name."

"Big deal. He worked for Ponti and the don let him do what he wanted on his estates. Why don't you check with Lorenzo himself?"

"You know what Ponti would tell us," Homer said.

"Yeah, he's not a nice guy like I am."

"Mr. Hammer," Homer insisted, "have you got any idea what your friend would transport in those trucks?"

"Of course," I told him.

They both edged forward on their chairs. "If you'd check those dates, it was when old Ponti was building his place up there in the mountains. Dooley was crating all the furnishings he was putting in there and hauling them up." Their expressions suddenly turned cold. "Why, do you think he was carting money someplace?"

They were lousy poker players. That's exactly what they had in mind. I was only guessing about when Ponti decided to move to the country, but it sounded like a good guess. If it had fallen to the don to hide the great pile of loot he'd need some kind of a cover story to do it and this would have been a logical one.

Neither one wanted another cup of coffee, so I let them leave and called Pat at his office. He chuckled when I told him what had happened, then asked what I was doing for lunch. I knew something was up by the way he said it and told him I'd meet him at his favorite pizza place at noon.

I had a single slice with coffee. Pat ate all the rest, washed it down with a cold Miller High-Life, then leaned back, satisfied. "Dooley has really got things rolling. This business with the families is nothing new. Our guys knew something was going on, but nobody was shooting at each other with any great regularity. . . ."

"What about the shoot-out at the dock?" I said sharply.

"That one was a total surprise. We never saw it coming. They put it down to a sudden animosity between the mobs, or something the young ones brought up. They couldn't find a reason for it and Ponti certainly didn't offer one. All he told us was 'You know how it is.' "

"Pat, you have something on your mind," I told him.

He waved for another cup of coffee. I shook my head. "For the past two years there has been some great familiarity between the young punks in the mob. It isn't that they have any great love for each other, just that they have something in common."

"Sure, the only thing that interests them is money."

"They've hired some fancy talent to do things for them. A lot of those kids are damn well schooled and know where to look for specialized help."

"But there's nothing you can charge them with," I stated.

"Right."

His coffee came and he tore open a couple packets of Sweet 'N Low and dropped the contents in.

"But we know where they have an office full of top of the line computer equipment. We staked the place out for three months and have a total of twenty-seven upper-echelon mobsters who have been there. We never knew why, but we have enough supposition to get a friendly judge to sign an order that allows us to search the place."

"Pat, you're not supposed to be telling me this."

"I know, pal, but it was you, me and Dooley before and no matter how you cut it, you're in this too."

"When are you going to hit that place?"

"No way you can tag along, Mike."

"Then how am I in it?"

"In spirit, pal. You can read about it in the papers."

"The feds going in?"

"Can't keep them out."

"But you have the search warrant."

"Sure, and we're scratching backs too."

I said, "When do I get the details, Pat?"

"As soon as it's not classified." He picked up his cup and finished the coffee. "Wondering why I'm telling you this much?"

I nodded. "As a matter of fact, I am."

Pat wiped his mouth and stood up. "I'm curious to see what you're going to do."

I said, "Oh," paid the bill, and told him so long outside the diner.

Willie-the-Actor was a little skinny guy with a strange kid-like voice, a deep love for any kind of booze, and no money at all. The job I held out for him was easy enough to do and meant a whole week in a bar if he could handle his money properly. It took a whole morning to get the scene staged properly and when I was sure he had it, we got in a cab, went to the address that I knew and made a call from a cellular phone.

He didn't know who he was talking to, but he said it fast and clearly, sounding like a twelve-year-old street kid half out of breath and real excited. He didn't even wait for the person on the other end to answer him. He said, "Ugo . . . Ugo . . . that you? You know that place where you guys meet? Some guy is watching it. I think he's gonna bust in there. I had to let you know cause we're kind of neighbors. You better get over here, Ugo." He stopped a moment and I could hear shouting in the phone, then he said, "Gee, he's lookin' over this way. I gotta go."

When he hung up I handed him his pay, let him get out of sight around the corner and went back to my cab. We didn't have to wait very long. Ugo Ponti came out of the garage under his house in the dark blue Buick and took off with a screeching of his wheels. My driver followed him without any difficulty at all. In New York there are cabs all over the city and one seems to look just like another. Twice we rode right alongside him and I got a good look at the glowering face of the prince of the local family.

We got down to Greenwich Village where new businesses have renovated the dilapidated old area and breathed new life into it. There was room at the curb for his car so he parked and hopped out. I paid off the cabby down the block, saw Ponti scan the street then enter a narrow alley between two buildings and disappear. The doorway was there, a heavy wooden leftover from a different century. The lock had been replaced with a good model, but one I could handle, so I just backed off, waited inside the lobby of a publishing firm until I saw Ugo step out, maddeningly puzzled, his face tight with anger. He looked around, shook his head and went back to his car, probably silently cursing the "kid" who had recognized him and passed on a bad tip to him.

The lock was as easy as I expected and I closed the door behind me, locking it again. I was in a stairwell with wide, old-fashioned treads and an ornately carved banister leading to the upper floors. I didn't have to go higher than the second. A pile of empty cardboard boxes and assorted trash blocked the way so I used my tools on the lock in the door to my left. Enough light came in from the old round window in the wall to let me see what I was doing and in two minutes I was inside.

Here I could use the lights. The windows were completely blacked out so that whatever was done here was done in secret. The tables were made of plywood on sawhorses, cheap chairs and soda boxes were used for chairs, and cardboard cartons were the containers for all the paper that ran through the computers and copiers that lined the room. There was a fortune in electronics and exotic machinery in every available space, and from the paper residue it had been in constant use.

There was nothing I could understand. I took out a good ten feet of paper, rolled it up and stuffed it in my pocket. Maybe somebody else could decipher the numbers. What I wanted to find was the material they were using for their computations. There were two filing cabinets. One held replacement tapes and copier paper, the other a set of repair tools and some replacement parts. Twice, I made a circuit of the room, poking into anything that might contain what I wanted. Nothing. I finally got it when I noticed the phones beside each one of the computer stations. They weren't taking any chances at all. They simply called out to another location to get their input material, reducing the odds of somebody getting wise.

I was all set to leave when I heard the stairs outside creak. I flipped the lights off, then squeezed in behind a four-drawer filing cabinet just before a key went into the lock and the door opened. The .357 came in first with Ugo right behind it and Howie Drago backing him up with an automatic in his fist.

Howie closed the door, then fanned out a little from Ugo and surveyed the room inch by inch. I was in a darkened corner and didn't move, so his eyes went right past the cabinets. Six feet away Ugo was doing the same thing, seemingly disappointed because they hadn't surprised anybody.

Finally Howie said, "You think that tip was square?"

"It was from a kid and they're not gonna make up stories like this."

"So you're like a hero to him, huh?"

"Why not? All the kids know who I am."

Howie wasn't sure at all. "What the hell was a kid doing over here?"

He got a disgusted sneer from Ugo for that one. "You think the kids don't follow me around? They know where I go to eat, the joints where I hang out—"

"That's not here, boss."

"It don't surprise me none, but I'll check it out."

"Tell me, why would anybody want to break in this place? There's nothin' here they could understand. The guys take all the books with them when they leave."

"If they saw this equipment being delivered here," Ugo told him, "and they knew the place was empty most of the time, this would be like a candy store for some druggie. They could even peddle the phones."

"I thought you was gonna get rid of this stuff."

"We are. Patterson's on it now. He has a truck coming in this week. They proved that the cash is missing, but they still don't know where. We paid a lot of idiots for nothin'."

Both of them were still moving while they talked, cautiously peering under the tables and kicking at piles of discarded waste. Ugo was the closest and his frustration was making him more nervous with every step. He was going to be damn sure nobody else was here and I knew he'd see the filing cabinet was out far enough from the wall to hide somebody behind it.

I stayed as immobile as I could. Ugo was getting close. I could hear his footsteps, the impact when his shoe booted something aside, then he was right up to the cabinet and he stopped dead. He saw the possible area, the only place in the room that could conceal a person and he was about to earn his bones once more.

It was too bad he was right-handed. Had he shifted the .357 to his other hand and come around the corner he would have nailed me, but he led with a stiffened right arm and I had twisted the rod out of his fingers before he knew what had happened, spun him around and held the muzzle of his own gun to the back of his neck. His breath was sucked in and he couldn't even talk, but I could smell the fear that oozed out of him and knew when he wet his pants.

When Howie saw Ugo standing there with the fear painted on his face and a forearm at his neck he stiffened momentarily until he saw the gun come away from Ugo's head and level directly at his face. And it was a big gun. It was the biggest S&W that they made and looked even bigger with all that nickel plating on it.

I said, "Drop the piece, Howie." My voice was nice and cold.

The automatic clattered to the floor. He kicked it away without being asked. He hadn't seen my face yet and didn't place my voice.

I said, "Turn around." He barely moved, so I thumbed the hammer back on the .357 and his face went white when he heard the click. He turned around then. "Walk backward over to me." His feet took little tiny steps as though he was forcing them to go in the wrong direction. I had him stop when he reached the spot I wanted, then cranked down on Ugo's neck so he couldn't move and slammed the gun against the side of Howie's skull. He went straight down like a puppet when you cut the strings and Ugo almost did the same thing when his knees gave way. I moved the gun back to his head again and felt his body begin to twitch. Ugo Ponti was looking down his own black alley.

There was no sense trying to change the tone of my voice. I just changed the tempo and volume when I said, "So your inheritance is down the drain, kiddo. Even the computer whiz kids don't know where it went. No transactions, no deposits . . . just a big nothing." I let my words sink in, let him measure the caliber of my voice. "But I'm going to find it, Ugo baby, only first you're going to tell me something."

His head bobbed against my arm and I loosened the hold enough so he could speak. Down at his feet Howie Drago's head was leaking blood that had pooled in the dirt of the floor and it was hard to tell if he were dead or alive.

Ugo waited for me to ask him what I wanted to know, hoping he'd be able to satisfy me with an answer of sorts. I said, "Who set up the hit on your old man at the piers last February?"

The consternation made him twitch again. It was a question he never expected at all and he fumbled for words. "It . . . was Azi."

"Azi's dead, kiddo. Who was helping him?"

"Reevo . . . Andy Reevo. He's from the family in Jersey."

"He's dead too, Ugo."

Ugo was running scared now, his words starting to choke him. "I . . . can't help it. The two of them . . . they planned it . . ."

"How did you know about it?"

"I . . . I heard them talking."

"You could have told the don, kiddo." I let him feel a nudge from the .357 and he tensed again.

"The old man . . . never would've believed me."

And he was right there. Azi was his pet, but the old don had sensed a loosening of the bonds and prepared for the eventuality of being set up. He could have even figured it out in advance. That lost money could do all sorts of things to family relationships.

I eased the gun away from Ugo's skin and let it run down his back, pressing against his spine. His mind was wondering if he'd feel the shot, cursing himself for not wearing body armor, not knowing whether or not to hope he'd die fast, but realizing that, if anything took out his spinal cord he was going to be strapped in a wheelchair for a long time. No parties, no broads, no booze, and just maybe somebody he kicked around might come up and plant a slug right in his face where he could see it coming.

Before he could faint on me I belted him in the head with his own gun and let him drop right on top of Howie. The blood from the gash above his temple mingled with the puddle on the floor and they were going to be a couple of real soreheads in the morning. I picked up the automatic and stuck it in my belt with Ugo's .357.

Pat could do a ballistics check on them both and maybe get some brownie points if they had been used in a crime scene earlier.

Downstairs Ugo's car was at the curb and I looked at the license plate. The first three numbers were 411.

NO GUNS HAD GONE OFF, but the nervous excitement of having Ugo and Howie Drago almost nail me had started a reaction inside my guts and I felt the little needles of pain begin to stab in sensitive places and knew that those needles would turn into great spikes of red-hot iron, and if I didn't stop it they would become killers. I took two of the pills Dr. Morgan had given me, eased myself onto the couch and stretched out. For ten minutes, the pain got bigger and broader, then gradually began to subside until it was localized at the wound in my side. I pulled up my shirt and stared at the bandage. It had turned a watery red.

Very gently, I pulled the phone over to me and dialed the number of Morgan's hotel. He was in and I told him what happened. His bedside manner had gotten a little better. He didn't get on my case at all. I called down to Bill Raabe and told him to come up and let the doctor in. I was okay, but didn't want to get up. There was no telling what he might give me that would make me sleep, so I called Pat and told him about the guns I had confiscated. He said he'd pick them up later. I told him to get them from Bill at the security desk because I was feeling lousy.

It took thirty minutes for the doctor to get to my apartment. Morgan took a look at me, shook his head and got my shirt off. He had Bill get some hot water and towels, then stuck a needle in my arm. Whatever it was, it eased any pain from stripping the bandage off. He washed and medicated the area and let Bill dispose of the discard. When I saw his face I knew he was beginning to realize what kind of a business I was in. He wiped the sweat from his upper lip, took the guns I had rolled up in a newspaper and went back downstairs.

Dr. Morgan said, "You're not going to be able to take much more of this, you know?"

I blinked once and he grinned at me.

"How long will it take, Mike?"

This time I didn't blink. I simply shrugged.

"Is the end in sight?"

I blinked twice. *No.*

"Will it be . . . dangerous?"

I nodded.

He nodded back. "You can call me anytime. I won't be going anyplace." He paused and pulled my shirt down over the fresh bandage. "You know how a cat is supposed to have nine lives, Mike?"

I blinked again. *Yes.*

"Well, if you were a cat, I'd say that you had already used up seven of them." His eyes bored into mine. "Get the picture?"

I blinked once, and this time my eyelids stayed closed. Whatever he had injected me with had really taken hold.

I heard him get up and the door click behind him when he left.

Something cool was on my forehead and there was an odd warmth next to me. I let my eyes open slowly, squinting at the muted light coming in the window. The small throb in my side made me remember times of sharper pains and a feeling of relief stirred me into a new wakefulness.

I raised my hand and felt my forehead, picking the damp washcloth off. Then the warmth next to me stirred and said, "It's about time you woke up."

Velda had a blanket over her, but she was fully dressed. Her makeup was smeared and her hair was messed up, yet she was totally beautiful. "You'll do anything to get in bed with me," I said.

"Even marry you if I have to."

"Now you have to. Did I snore?"

"No, but you talked up a storm. Nothing made much sense except going upstate. You've had that on your mind since Friday."

"Friday? What day is this?"

"Sunday morning. The doctor and I have been pampering you like a baby for a day and a half. If your face is sore it's because I shaved you."

I flexed my cheeks, but nothing hurt. She had done a good job. "What about my . . . *other* necessities?"

"Sorry. I left the room and the doctor went through all that with you. I would have been glad to help but didn't think it was my place." Then she added, "Yet."

"Did Morgan leave any instructions?"

"Nothing you'd like to hear. He said he's told you about all he can. You're the one who has to be choosy now." She leaned over and nipped my ear with her teeth.

"I'm going to bring you some coffee, your pills, then I'm going to take a shower and get dressed."

"You have your clothes here too?"

"I picked them up while the doctor was here."

For half an hour I came back to normal with some rye bread toast and coffee, letting it settle down easy. After the second cup I swung my feet over the side of the bed and pushed myself upright. My body felt as though I had been through a barroom brawl when it hadn't been like that at all. Hell, I had been shot before. It had hurt and put me in the sack for a couple of days until the healing got underway, but there were no aftereffects. I touched the scars that were like dimpled marks, suddenly remembering that those wounds were made in muscle tissue and not in the vital soft working parts of the anatomy.

The last time I had been back on the streets in five days and was jogging two weeks later. Two punks thought I was a drunk and tried to mug me. I put them on their backs right after the first one tried to sucker punch me and belted them silly before I let them lie down. No aftereffects then.

Now I had to get up slowly and not walk too fast. Now I was getting in my own way. Velda came out of the bathroom and seemed to read my mind. "It's only temporary, Mike. The doctor said that in another month you'll be completely mobile."

I said something under my breath.

"You ready for a shower?" she asked.

I nodded.

"Dr. Morgan left a plastic covering to tape over your bandage while you get wet. Want me to do it for you?"

She was quick and efficient and, when she was done, pointed me toward the shower. "I think you can take care of the rest alone."

"Gee, thanks," I told her.

"We'll save the good parts for later," she said.

Sitting at the kitchen table nice and clean, pants pressed and shirt crisp and ironed, I felt like a new person. Good to look at, but not ready for action. Velda had a fresh pot of coffee made and after she filled the cups she sat opposite me and opened a spiral-bound notebook filled with notations.

"Those researchers did a pretty cool job. You want me to read off the figures?"

"No, just estimate. Give me the round picture."

"Okay. These are from the years you selected. Drugs: the total confiscated by American agents were worth two hundred million. They estimate that fifty times that much went on the streets. It could have been more. These figures never changed for nine years. In fact, it was supposed that the importers were getting ahead of the narcotic agencies. The final figures are in the billions."

"How many?"

"From ten to thirty. There's no way of telling."

"Money laundering adds another ten billion. Get into the union business and the costs that get laid on commercial industries from mob activities and you got a few more. Want me to go on?"

"What's your opinion, kitten?"

"That eighty-nine-billion-dollar figure you gave was light. You know what the big catch is, Mike?"

"Yeah, where to put it if you take it out of circulation."

"And that leaves your friend Dooley."

"He used those trucks and those cartons for something," I said.

"Pat checked that one out while you were sleeping."

"Oh?"

"Those trucks were seen working in and around Ponti's

estate, all right. He moved up a whole houseful of things for his boss. Then he brought in sod and lumber. It sure looks legitimate."

"What's that saying? Looks can be deceiving. All that work could have been a good cover for other work."

She knew what I was thinking. "You up to it?" she asked me.

"As ready as I'll ever be," I told her.

Nobody had been near my car since I parked it. All the telltales I had placed were still intact and the light dusting of carbon under the car showed no signs of being disturbed. I put our bags in the trunk, backed out of my area and pulled out onto the street.

I didn't bother to look for a tail. If Homer Watson was as good as they said he was, he'd have planned a nice box for me. There would be no single car chase. His badge carried enough authority to enlist any police forces he needed so he could let them do the hard work while he covered the rear, staying in touch on the radio.

But the rabbit always has a hole to get into ahead of the fox.

Bill Raabe waited in the garage entrance and when he saw the green *Milos* truck coming up the street he waved me out at the right moment and I got in front of it, so that when it stalled and stopped traffic I got to the corner, turned north, went one block west and turned left again for a single block, made another left, and I was back on my own block again when I got back in my own garage. "How'd it go?" I yelled out.

"Mike, it was real funny. Some pudgy guy in a blue suit hit the roof. No kidding. I thought he was gonna pass out. He was screaming into a walkie-talkie unit, then the truck got started up and pulled away. That guy hopped in his car and damned if he didn't get stopped again by another car pulling out of the garage down the street."

Velda glanced at me, her expression grim. "Think we made it, Mike?"

I said, "The first pickup car was probably two blocks down, but we only went one block. I didn't spot a tail after our first turn. Right now they're trying to figure out what happened."

"How've you got it planned?" Bill asked me.

"I'm going straight across town and pick up the highway to the bridge."

"Okay, pal. Good luck."

I eased out into traffic, got behind some taxies and did just that. Velda and I kept a tight watch on what was behind us and when we hit the highway we both breathed a sigh of relief.

On the other side of the George Washington Bridge I headed for Route 9W and took the scenic trip up along the Hudson River, and when we passed through Newburgh I looked at the map and pinpointed the spot where Marcos Dooley kept his boat in the old days. It was still there, dilapidated and overgrown with weeds, but it had a pier and docking facilities for a half dozen boats and two well-used sailboats were still in the slips.

There was a sign outside the small house that read "James Bledsoe, Prop." The porch was apparently the office and living quarters were behind it. I knocked and heard somebody say he'd be right there, so we waited patiently until an old guy came hobbling out munching on an apple, his knobby knees sticking out of stained khaki shorts. "You don't look like boat people," the old guy said.

"We're not."

It didn't surprise him at all. He sat down on a box

behind an old table and laced his fingers together behind his head. "You don't want to rent a boat, do you?"

"Not today."

"Didn't think so."

"Mr. Bledsoe . . . did you know Marcos Dooley?"

His eye brightened and he took his hands down, leaning on his knees. "Sure did. We had a lot of good times together, us two. Haven't seen him for a few years."

"He's dead, Mr. Bledsoe."

"Damn." He frowned. "What happened?"

"He was murdered, but that's kind of an old story now. I understand he had a boat here. A Woolsey," I described.

"You mean a *Wheeler.* Woolsey and Wheeler were an old comedy team. Anyway, it's still here," he said. "It's all dried out and needs a lot of work on her, but if you got a few months and some money it can be done."

"I'd just like to see it."

"Pretty dirty out there."

"That's okay."

And he was right. The old barn held three antique boats with open seams, glass falling out of their frames and rust stains leaking from all exposed metal parts. Chocks held Dooley's boat upright, streamers of cobwebs and layers of dust making it look like the *Flying Dutchman.* The hatch cover was off and candy wrappers were scattered around.

"Kids," Bledsoe explained. "They come in here and play. I can't keep them out. At least they don't smoke or mess around with girls."

I pointed to a ladder that ran up the side. "Mind if I look around?"

"Be my guest."

The ladder was handmade, but sturdy enough. I went up slowly and threw a leg over the rail and got on the deck, brushing the cobwebs out of my face. Apparently the old man hadn't been up here in a long time. The kids must have had a ball seeing how much damage they could do. They had broken into the small cabin and pulled out anything that came loose. Light fixtures were smashed and dried turds made a mess in the ceramic head. The wheel in the cabin was intact, being a good plaything, but behind it were only holes where instruments had been screwed into the mahogany. The metal body of an early fish finder was smashed and twisted and next to it a loran unit had been gouged apart. Old Dooley would really have turned green if he could see his boat now.

I shook my head in absolute disgust and looked over the mahogany dashboard where the kids had scratched their names and almost turned away when I saw something else that was written there. Not a scrawl or a scratch, but six numbers carefully inscribed with an awl so they couldn't be rubbed out.

They were the same six numbers Dooley had given to be put on his urn, his supposed military serial number! Damn, those were not ID digits, they were latitude and longitude markers to a spot Dooley had wanted to be found in case he was put out of action.

I climbed down, brushed myself off and told Bledsoe there wasn't much we could do with the boat, but we'd let him know.

"What should I do with it?" he wanted to know.

"Dooley had a son. . . ."

"Yeah, I remember that little kid."

"He'll probably want to see it, so it's up to him now."

The old man made sucking sounds around his false teeth and bobbed his head. "It's okay by me. Sure was sorry to hear that Dooley is gone. Think they'll get who killed him?"

I grinned. I wasn't looking at him, but what he saw was enough. I knew my teeth were showing and I could feel the tight lines in my face. When I moved my eyes and stared at him he seemed to recoil. "They'll get him," I said.

Velda hooked her arm in mine and tugged me away. We walked through the grass and up the driveway to where we had left the car. We walked slowly and she didn't say anything at all. She didn't like what she had seen on my face either. Before I got behind the wheel I took off my jacket and laid it in the back seat. I unbuttoned my shirt and pulled the collar apart and Velda said, "What kind of underwear do you call that?"

I opened another button so she could see what it was. "Bulletproof, kitten. It goes all the way down to my hips and covers the hole in my side. I don't even want to get bumped hard in a grocery store."

"Just stay away from its primary use," she warned me.

"Gotcha, doll."

When we got to Albany I stopped at two places specializing in marine supplies. They both sold loran equipment, but had no way of determining where the lat-lon numbers I gave them were located. Off shore they would have no trouble, but up here in mountain country they were at a loss. In the last place one of the salesmen said, "Why don't you try a survey outfit? They lay out land parcels like that."

"Good idea. You know any outfit I can call?"

He gave me McClain and Leeds, dialed the number and handed over the phone.

The guy was young, friendly, and told me to come on over and he'd give me a map with the location I wanted.

Cheery guy. You could tell you were out of the big city. I thanked the salesman and got back in the car.

Johnny Leeds met us at the door, glad to see somebody from the Big Apple. We had to tell him what was new on Broadway, where the latest *in* spots were and how much an apartment with a decent address cost. I told him he didn't even want to know and to stay happy up here with trees and grass. Finally he agreed with me and we got down to my problem.

When I showed him the numbers he made a face like they were familiar to him, looked up something in a book, then waved us to a wall map. "That wasn't hard," he said.

"You know that place?"

"Sure. Everybody does. There was an old bootlegger named Harris . . ."

"Slipped Disk," Velda offered.

"Yeah, that's him. He ran a bootleg operation out of there during prohibition. Not much left up there now. The big house rotted out a long time ago and some old caretaker lives in an outbuilding. Once in a while he cuts some choice slate out of there. You looking to buy the place?"

"It's possible."

Leeds smiled gently at the two city slickers and warned us, "That's a depressed area if you want to start a business."

"How about starting a family?" I grinned back. Velda's mock punch in my arm was soft, but I felt it.

He looked at Velda appreciatively and said, "Now there's a great idea." He turned and went to a rack of road maps, pulled one out, traced out the route from where we were right up to the Harris property.

Driving there wasn't that simple. Where the state ran out of roads the county took over, and when townships wanted to maintain them, the county nodded an okay, and when nobody used them anymore except an old recluse the township let them have their way. After four wrong turns we found the narrow, single-lane dirt road that twisted and turned through the trees toward the rise of the Appalachian Mountains that marked the area.

Jammed in a ditch where it had skidded off the road was the wreckage of an old truck, two stout pine trees keeping it from sliding further down the slope. Velda said, "Did you see that?"

I nodded. "That was an old chain-driven Mack truck."

"What would it be doing here?"

"Those were the major workhorses of the day. Not fast, but they sure could haul a payload. This is slate country, remember. You'd need a Mack to get that stuff out of here."

"Or booze, right?"

She had a point there. "Right," I said.

The old estate of Slipped Disk Harris came on us like a sudden sunrise. We went around a turn and there were no more trees, just a big empty field on the edge of an overpowering mountainside with three old buildings nestling in the shadows. Small hills of grey slag made mounds on the acreage, insolently decorated with purple thistles. The single roadway branched out into five different directions, all but one in total disrepair, so I stayed on the passable one, which brought me to a weatherworn building that had been patched and repatched, but still looked livable. There was a brick chimney running up the side, and although no smoke came out, there was a shimmer of heat distortion against the clouds, so I knew someone was there.

Rather than take a chance on stirring up some irritable old mountaineer waving a shotgun, I beeped the horn and waited. The screen door with paint so thick you couldn't see through it whipped open and the mountaineer was there, all right, old, but smiling and not at all irritable. "Y'all step down and come right in," he yelled. His voice was cackly, but happy. "Sure good to see some company. Saw you comin' a mile away and put on coffee."

Velda slid out and introduced herself. "You sure a looker," the old man said. "I'm just Slateman. Got a real name, but nobody calls me that." He took my hand too, shook it and squinted up at me. "Do I know you?"

"We never met, Slateman. First time I've been up this way."

"You an actor? Got a TV, ya know."

"Nope."

"Man, only actors got good-lookin' women like yours here. What do ya do?"

"What I want to do is see Slipped Disk's old operation."

"Ah, yes," Slateman said. "You're a writer, that's what. About every two years some newspaper guy or a book writer comes up here to see what it was all about. See, I knew I could figure you out. This lady your whatchamacall it?"

I nudged Velda with my elbow. "You may call her that," I said. Velda nudged me back and her fingernails bit warningly into my arm.

The place was clean and neat, but a decorator's nightmare. The walls were lined with pink insulation, ballooning out between the studs, and cattails and dried leaves stuffed into old bottles prettied up the rough board shelving. I pointed to a large multicolored arrangement that exploded out of a coffee can and asked, "What is that?"

Velda was the one to say, "Queen Anne's lace, dyed and dried. We used to do that with food coloring when we were kids. I haven't seen that for a long time."

Slateman was beaming at her. Apparently until now nobody had appreciated his handiwork. "Did it all myself," he stated proudly. "Nothin' to it, really. What I like is those cattails. Sometimes I light 'em up and the smoke keeps the bugs away. Everything's good for something, ya know." He got the pot from the woodstove and poured the coffee into three mismatched cups on the table. "Only got sugar here. Got no cow and the store's too far away. Couldn't milk a cow anyway."

So we talked country talk until we finished the coffee, then Slateman stood up said, "You want to see where Ol' Slipped Disk kept the stuff, right?"

"You got it."

"Better get your cameras then."

For a minute I felt stupid, then Velda winked at me and went out to the car. She came back with a small 35mm Minolta that had a flash attachment and seemed very professional about it. Slateman got an oversized flashlight with a strap that slung over one shoulder and led us through the house and out the back door.

There was a story about everything, the age of the farm, the history of the big barn where Harris had kept the trucks, the old well that was sixty feet deep and still filled with clear, cold water from an underground stream. Velda wanted to know how they dug it out and Slateman took ten minutes to explain it to her in detail.

After that we followed a path to the ridge of bushes, then around them to where the ground soared up like an overturned teacup and melted into the mountain proper behind it. We could have missed it if we had been looking ourselves, but when Slateman laughed at us and pointed we saw the cleft in the side of the hill. He pulled a rack of bushes aside and there was an opening a man on horseback could go through. "Used to have a big wooden barn door here," Slateman explained. "Couldn't see it, of course. Always kept it properly covered with real growth. A truck could go in and out easy."

He led the way, flicking on his torch, and we stayed close behind. It was a great natural cave, cool and dry. The dirt under our feet was well packed and the space so big that we could only see one wall to our left.

Velda's voice had a quaver to it. "Any bats?"

"No bats," Slateman reassured her. "Some caves have 'em, but this one don't. Can't figure it out."

We walked until we reached the perimeter of it and followed the curve of the walls around. Even after all these years you could tell what had been here. They had shipped booze in wood boxes then, and some were still there. Old tools and the remains of a truck seat were like artifacts in an antique shop. At the back side we had to circle around a heap of old boulders Slateman said had come down from the wall and overhead years ago. He flashed the light above us to make sure we were still safe. Boulders didn't bother Velda at all. It was just the bats that bothered her. She made Slateman cover the entire room with his light before she was really satisfied. Velda kept popping pictures until she ran out of film, but by then we had completed the tour and were back at the entrance again.

"How much did he have here, Slateman?"

"Plenty, I'd guess," the old man said. "I wasn't here in the real old days, but they told me this place was packed. I finally figured out what he did, ya know."

"What was that?"

"Old Harris, he stored it up here. He didn't just fill orders from the big city. Hell no, he kept buying and storing and when an order came in he took it right out of his supply here. He'd wait until the coast was clear, then bring in his trucks. Smart man, him." He said it with admiration in his tone. "Gov'ment never could catch up with him."

"Too bad prohibition went out of style," I remarked.

Slateman chuckled. "Nah, not with him. He hung on to his stockpile and sold it later down in New York. Raised hell, ya know. Bought it a lot cheaper in the old days. No tax, no nothing. He made a bundle before he died. All gone now."

Velda and I looked at each other. It had all been so simple. For Harris, anyway. For us it was just a big, empty cave of dust and memories and a little old guy glad to have some city slickers visit him. Velda reloaded the camera again and shot some footage around the property while the sun was still up, then stowed the camera away. We told Slateman so long, got back in the car and started down the single-lane road.

We turned south on the main highway and stopped at the first diner we came to, went in and ordered up sausage and pancakes with plenty of real maple syrup and mugs of steaming coffee. This time I had it with Sweet 'N Low.

Halfway through the pancakes, Velda said, "What did we miss, Mike?"

I shook my head in annoyance. "Dooley went through a lot of trouble to plant those numbers. He wanted me to find them and to position them. Okay, so I did both, but they were dead ends."

"Could someone else have gotten there before us?"

"How? Dooley hasn't been dead that long."

"He must have been expecting to get killed, that's for sure. He etched those numbers on his boat long before he died, so he had something planned 'in case.' "

"And he got 'in case,' all right." I washed down my last

forkful of supper and waved for another coffee. "You know what the big bug is . . . I was expecting that latitude and longitude to lie right on Ponti's estate. That's where Dooley did all his work, so why the switch to Slipped Disk Harris?"

"Weren't they great friends?"

"According to Dooley's kid, but we never looked into that end."

"Why not?"

"Because everything was handed to us on a platter. We had the end in our hands without knowing the beginning. Eighty-nine billion dollars was stashed away waiting to be found and the government and the hoods were looking for it too. Somebody finally figured out it was Don Ponti who had corralled the loot. His own kid made the connection and tried to set him up. Well, Azi Ponti made his exit with a .45 slug in his head and now we have Ugo to contend with. That little sucker can still pull a lot of weight with the family, but not as much as the don."

Velda sat there pensively a minute or so, idly tapping her teeth with a thumbnail. "Mike . . . Don Ponti was a pretty hot-headed guy, wasn't he?"

"Yeah, when he was young."

"Two years ago they had that rumble with the strikers on that building project. He was there trying to break heads until his men hustled him away."

"Nothing ever came of that, Velda."

"He could still get mad. He could still swing a bat. You think he's changed now?"

I said, "I doubt it."

"Then how come he's laying low? How come he hasn't sent anybody out to put a hit on you? After all, you went putting an arm on his people. You challenge Ugo and

Patterson and Drago for starters . . . he knows your connection with Dooley . . . yet he lets you alone."

"Damn, Velda, you talk just like a street cop."

"I carry a gun too. Now tell me, Mike."

"He's waiting to see how far I get."

"Go on."

"If Dooley's lead is any good and I uncover it, he guns us down and takes over."

"No . . . he can't just take over. The cache is too big. Physically, I mean. He just wipes you out and he has it all to himself. Right now he's a little worried because you have Uncle Sam's men on your tail too, and he doesn't want them pointing at him. He doesn't want Pat to roust him either. No, he's waiting for you to make a move."

She had it pretty well figured out. "If I decided to visit Ponti's place to see where Dooley came into the picture, and Ponti was waiting for me, I could become the victim of an accidental shooting or a supposed intruder he thought was trespassing."

"He'd think of something good."

"Ponti doesn't live too far from here," I reminded her. "He and Harris were friends and in the same business."

"And you are going to pay him a visit."

"What do you think, doll?"

"I think we ought to sleep on it."

The desk clerk at the Cinnamon Motel had given me an odd look when I signed in for two rooms. Not that I could blame him. The bumper stickers and license plates of the parked cars seemed to indicate that it was a fairly popular local rendezvous and he couldn't understand why I was putting Velda in a separate compartment.

At seven-thirty I was up and hungry, banging on her door. She opened it before I could rap it the third time, standing there in mock anger, dressed in a black jumpsuit with a greenish sheen woven into it. On most girls it would be a casual hiking outfit, but on her it looked like it was painted on.

She said, "It's about time you came home. You ought to be ashamed, staying away all night—"

"You going out like that?" I interrupted.

Her eyebrows went up. "Mike . . ." her voice seemed annoyed, "this is the way I'm made. I have no engineering, internal or external, built into me. I'm sorry, but . . ."

I let a laugh out. "Don't be sorry, doll. Let everybody else be sorry."

For that remark she blew me a kiss, grabbed a small handbag and shut the door.

IT WAS LIKE BEING BACK in the army again, scouting the details of Lorenzo Ponti's estate. We had parked a good mile away and worked our way through the brush and clusters of trees until we came over a rise and saw the don's vacation home. It wasn't a pretentious place at all, large enough for a big family with plenty of open ground space for a couple of football fields with stadium lights for night games of softball if you wanted. Or a deadly area for an approaching enemy to try to cross if he was going to initiate an attack on the house.

At strategic points around the building were cleverly designed floral beds, raised a good three feet at the center with rocks arranged for protected shooting, but obscuring a decent view of the premises from anybody approaching. The main door was formidable in size and construction, the hinges huge, the structure being decorative as well as useful.

Velda handed me the binoculars. "I don't see a thing," she said.

"That's because you're a city girl." We moved a little to the right and I focused in on a shadow between one of the hills and the house, then handed the glasses back and told her what to look for.

Finally she got it. "I see the shadow . . . if that's what you mean."

"That's what I mean, all right. Now, what's causing it?"

She checked the sunlight and shadow from the trees and shook her head. "Nothing."

"Right. That shadow is a shallow ditch. It leads to a window at ground level of the building. Take another look."

She peered through the glasses again, then said, "You should have been at the Alamo. We would've won."

"Kitten, I would have been outside that church long before Santa Anna got there. Now, if you can spot them, there are four depressions like that so you could go out from or into the main building."

"I see one to the right."

"Can you see the windows?"

"Only the outline. They have no glass in them."

"And they'll be barricaded. If you notice up under the eaves there are some decorative wooded sections with a few slots in them. Get the glasses on them while there's still some light."

When she located them she studied them carefully. She handed the glasses back to me with a serious frown tugging at her eyes. "Boss, you surprise me," she said. "For someone straight out of New York . . ."

"I didn't say I grew up there, kitten."

"Okay, what are those things? They don't make sense to me."

"The don's got a place that's *real* early American. He's

got a damn fortress there and we've only seen the front side. These slotted jobs are shooting stations too. You slide open the slots and you can aim down at the enemy from high ground, and whatever he has for weapons must be pretty substantial."

Her voice was incredulous. "And you're taking them on?"

"I didn't say that either." I gave her a small grin. "Besides, I wouldn't be surprised if all that ground was seeded with remote-activated land mines."

"Why remote?"

"So you couldn't set them off accidentally."

"Who would want to go out there at all?"

"Nobody who lived in the house, that's for sure."

I handed her the glasses and she packed them back in her bottomless purse. "You know, Mike," she said to me, "I think I enjoyed this stuff more back in the city. You don't get hung up on thistle bushes and briars, or get stuck by pine needles." She pushed a branch away from her face and said a low, "Damn!"

"Quit complaining," I told her.

"And there aren't any bats in the city."

"There aren't any bats here either," I reminded her.

"Why weren't any in the cave at Harris' place? On TV they always come swooping out of old caves at sundown."

"Look, if you want bats, I'll find you some. Don't you know that—"

"They don't get caught in your hair," she finished for me. "Yes, I know they are naturally radar guided and have nothing to do with vampires and keep the insect population in control, but the damn things scare me and please let me have my idiosyncrasies."

"Okay, but out here in the brush look out for snakes. This is copperhead heaven."

She stopped dead in her tracks and stared at me. "Did

you have to say that? I'm terrified of snakes. If you want to carry me . . ."

"Honey . . ." I tried to placate her ". . . what would I know? I didn't grow up here."

There was a long pause. "Mike, do you know how to kill a snake?"

"Sure. Turn a mongoose on him."

"That's what I thought," she said sourly. "Why don't you just keep walking and keep quiet."

It took the better part of an hour to see the don's house from all angles. A lot of thought had gone into its construction, even the placement of the outbuildings, which could well have tunnel connections with the big house. Back in the early thirties this setup would have been perfect for the vacation quarters of the head of a family. Or even as the seat of the organization. It would be totally self-sufficient, with water, food and disposal naturally taken care of. They could sit inside their snug fortress and nobody could get to them at all. Not without dying, that is.

But Babylon had been like that once too. Giant stone walls encased it, a river ran through it, but the Babylonians threw a party the night the Mede and Persian armies cut off the water flow from the Euphrates River and thousands of armed men walked through the great opening in the wall and slaughtered all the drunks.

We had just reached the cover of the trees when a black limousine came around the curve and drove up to the main entrance. I snapped my fingers for the glasses and Velda handed them to me. I saw Patterson get out from the driver's seat, open the back door and help Don Ponti out. The old man was dressed in country clothes this time: khaki pants, rolled up high enough to show tan boots, and a plaid shirt with a cowboy vest over it. He carried what looked like a sheepskin jacket to keep the mountain chill off. The front door opened and a bald, stout middle-aged guy came out, bowing and scraping to the don, hauling his bags out of the limo's trunk, then leading the way back into the house, standing aside at the door so the don could make his grand entrance. Patterson got back in the limo and circled the house to the garage area. He didn't come back, so he must have gone in through another entrance.

"What do you make of that?" Velda asked.

"He's up here for more than overnight. Those bags probably had personal items he likes to have around him. Clothes and everything else would be here."

"Wouldn't he have more of his men around him?"

"Wait, kitten. They'll be here."

Two men carrying shotguns came out of the woods, walking on either side of the drive. Another minute and two more limos eased into the area and we could see the white faces of the men behind the glass. Just as the cars reached the house another pair of men walked up. There were no shotguns this time. Both of them cradled assault rifles in their arms and their eyes searched every place an enemy could be. They didn't go in the house. They simply melted into the shadows and we couldn't see them at all.

Very carefully, we went back the way we had come. I was wondering why they didn't have a canine guard around, but maybe they felt safe enough as it was. In another hour we were back at the car and I picked up the road that led back toward the motel. Somehow Velda had managed to get the knots out of her hair and dry-brushed herself back to decency. But the way she fit into her jumpsuit sure turned heads at the Cinnamon Motel.

And I was glad she was a magnet for all those eyes, because one set belonged to Howie Drago and another to one of the don's soldiers. She must have picked up on it as soon as I did because without a word to them, she walked into the office of the motel and I knew she'd be leaving out the back door. Women don't like to leave their goodies behind them. She'd get in her room, grab her stuff and be expecting me to pick her up outside her door without a single break in routine. So I just pulled away as if I were only the driver, went down the drive onto the street, turned left back to the entrance and kept on going past the knot of Ponti's men and they didn't even recognize the second pass of the same car. I pushed the door open on the passenger side and Velda came out of her room, slid in with her canvas bag and, as I drove back to the road, casually tossed it on the backseat.

"I told the clerk we were leaving and gave him sixty bucks to cover tonight. I didn't bother to get a receipt."

"Just put it on the office expenses."

"Don't worry. I will," she said. "Now, what were those people doing there?"

"That's the only motel around here."

"I'm not going to come apart, Mike. They could have gone with Ponti like the others."

"Okay, he's got a rear guard. He has enough men in his private army to set up a roadblock wherever he wants around here."

"Mike . . . how would he know?"

The highway was directly ahead. So far there had been no attempt at an interception. I said, "The don's no dummy. This is where the thing started and it looks like it will end here too. Ponti didn't need any road maps. All he has to do is wait. He thinks that the only one who knows where eight-nine billion bucks are stashed is me. And by association, you."

"But we don't!"

"We still have an edge if he thinks so," I told her.

As we turned south on the highway she stared out the window. "How are you going to get into the house?"

"Ponti's going to invite me in."

"Mike . . ."

"You're not going with me, doll. I need somebody on the outside."

"You can have an . . . accident. . . ." Velda suggested, leaving the rest unsaid.

I tapped the cruise control button and kept the car on the posted limit. Civilization started to appear little by little and at the third turnoff I swung to the right and followed the road to the Hawthorn Motel that I had seen on a billboard a mile back.

This time the desk clerk was a pleasant-faced lady in her sixties and when I asked for two rooms she gave me a startled look and said, "Why?"

"Because we're not married yet."

Her eyebrows went up and she drew back a bit. "Well, I'll be darned. This her idea?" She gave Velda a disapproving look.

"No," I said, "it's mine. We're only engaged."

"Well, friend, you had better get ready for some practice time then. I have one room left and it's a double."

"Two beds?"

"Yes, why?"

"Ever see *It Happened One Night*?"

Velda was glaring at me when I took the keys. Her mouth was hiding a smile while her eyes were biting me. The desk clerk just shook her head, not able to figure me out. Now I was beginning to enjoy being a good guy.

Inside the room Velda said, "Do we really have to put up the walls of Jericho?"

"Not if you behave yourself."

I chased her into the shower and she came out beautifully dampened in a black nightgown. It was one of those accessories that had a specific purpose in mind, but from the look on her face it was like shooting blanks.

When I came out, teeth brushed, shaved and showered, in my fresh pajama bottoms, the single bed lamp was on very low and she waved me over to her side. "Do I get a good night kiss?"

I reached for her wrists and folded my fingers around them. She was silky to feel and she let me hold her arms down on either side of her head. She was beginning to understand the game now. The tip of her tongue traced a sparkling wetness across her lips and they parted as I bent over her. She was warm and lovely and that little bit of her that I touched was alive with suppressed fire. I could feel it and I could taste it. I pulled away reluctantly, then said softly, "I love you, kitten."

Her eyes told me all I wanted to know. I went to my own bed. There was another debt I owed to the army. It taught me how to sleep under any conditions.

When I gassed up the attendant directed me to a car rental spot and I got a Ford Mustang for Velda. There was a breakfast spot a block away so after we ate we tried to put it all together again. There were no new answers.

Then an answer walked in the door, looked around deliberately until he spotted us and came over to our table. Both of us had been around too long to seem surprised, so I said, "Sit down, Homer. You have breakfast yet?"

Homer Watson shook his head. "No, I thought I'd join you." He indicated he'd have what we had ordered and sat back smiling.

I didn't let him get in the first word. "You have any trouble locating us?"

"Just a little," he told me. "The federal government has fingers that reach into every nook and cranny of American life. You weren't hard at all."

"Oh?"

He made a wry face. "We can make immediate connections with any local police agency if we want lookouts. Knowing pretty well where this affair was taking you made it a lot easier. Of course, we knew you'd be getting another car, so calls went out to all rental agencies in the area and presto, an hour ago we knew where you were."

Velda leaned forward, her fingers laced together. "Do you mean that we have the entire United States government backing up a homicide investigation?"

That took him off his direct line of thought, making him frown a moment.

"Marcos Dooley," Velda reminded him. "He was murdered."

If he tried to make a wise remark he knew I was going to lay a fist right in his mouth and he stopped it before it was born. Instead, he said, "You know what I'm looking for."

"And what are we looking for, Homer?"

He took a deep breath and studied us with deliberate patience, as though we were being recalcitrant students. "Your secretary here made some interesting inquiries regarding funds obtained by the organized underworld."

"That was all public information, Mr. Watson," Velda said. "Printed periodicals."

"Two weren't. Computer information was tapped into that we had red-flagged."

"Sneaky, Homer," I said.

"Not really. Just a minute corner of our agency was involved to get this far. This is very amateur stuff for our bureau."

"Then why haven't you found what you're looking for?"

"We will."

"You can't," I said. "Hell, you don't even know what you're after."

His voice had a driven edge to it. "There are up to a hundred billion dollars of unreported, untaxed money . . ."

"Let's keep it around eighty-nine billion, Homer," I said softly.

Suddenly, his eyes came alive. "Damn it, Hammer, you know where it is." This time his voice was flushed and quiet. He was like a hunter who had spotted his deer and was taking a careful sight on its vital spot.

I said, "I only know some numbers, buddy."

"You can be arrested, you know."

"For what?"

"Withholding information."

"Drop dead, clown."

Muscles in his neck tightened, the cords standing out behind the fat. He didn't like the adjective at all. "Don't tempt me, Hammer. I could dream up a dozen charges real fast to put you in a cage for a few days."

"They'd have to be phony, wouldn't they?"

"Who cares?" he asked flippantly.

I looked at Velda with a small grin. "That all down on the recorder?"

She nodded. "Every word."

"I don't think you'll pull that stunt now, will you? Incidentally, you got a gun on you too?"

He looked at my hand hovering near the opening into my coat jacket, then at my eyes, and didn't like what he saw. "We have to be armed," he told me.

"That's nice to know." I didn't take my hand away until his two hands were flat on the table.

The waitress came with his breakfast and he made a

deliberate effort to get into it. I sipped at my coffee and watched him carefully, trying to get some mental background on where he stood. It was common knowledge that the government had been making a big effort to get inside the working of the Mafia. In some ways it was working. Overseas the bosses had been picked up and jailed, here the same thing had happened. But whether the government took them out or their own organization gunned them down, it didn't seem to matter at all. Someone else was ready and able to step right into the emptied position and a new don was born. Some of them were tough, some of them had sense, and some had both, but eventually they all become losers.

Along the line, some of them saw what was coming up and prepared for the occasion.

All that mattered was money. People could come and go, but the money was the constant. They'd fight over it, kill for it, but if the bosses could hide it where only *they* could get to it, their retirement could be secure and their position permanent. Trouble was, all the old dons were gone except Lorenzo Ponti. He should have had it, but a caretaker, a grass-cutter he employed to handle the loot, had screwed him royally.

"Watson," I said, "with all this supposed money somewhere, how come your bureau sends you out alone?"

Before he could answer I held my hand up. "Don't lie, pal. I could make a call to your department and see what's up. Or alert them to the whole package."

He swallowed, wiped his plate with a piece of toast and stuck it in his mouth. When he washed it down with coffee, he wiped his lips and said, "This has been a project of mine for ten years. The bureau chief assigned it to me."

"That's a long while, Homer."

"There never was a time limit on it. We had suspected

what was going on, but when the young turks started getting interested things picked up."

"No hard evidence?"

After a pause he said, "None."

"What put you on Dooley?"

"Just the fact that he worked for Ponti. He didn't seem to fit the profile of someone who would associate with a known mobster. Ponti didn't use casual help like that for very long or as intimately."

"You report all this?"

"Of course."

"And your superiors just brushed it aside as mere speculation."

He didn't want to admit it, but I was right.

"Well," he said, "it was speculative. Nobody seemed to believe the amounts I had told them, even though they had their own research to look at. The difficulty was they couldn't see the Mafia organizations hoarding that kind of loot. It had always gone somewhere—into casinos, businesses, union operations."

"So they left you out on your own all that time?"

"I am well paid."

"What made you tie it together?"

"You, Mr. Hammer." He leaned back in his chair and looked at me coolly. "When Marcos Dooley was shot down a memo reached me because I had made a notation about him on my report. What really alerted me was his asking only for you. I knew that this was one of those rare historical times when a door was opened and the end was right in sight."

"So you think he told me something," I stated.

"I know he told you something. You know where . . . was it eighty-nine? . . . billion dollars is hidden. Those are *billions,* Mr. Hammer. That's an incredible amount of money. That's big enough to take a big hunk out of this country's deficit. With it this country can—"

"Tell it to the politicians, Homer. I'm looking for a person who killed my friend."

A baffled hatred touched his eyes a second. He said, "Tell me this then, Mr. Hammer. You can tell the truth, can't you?"

"When necessary."

"Let this be necessary then."

"What, Homer?"

"Do you know *where* the money is?"

For a good three seconds I stared straight into his eyes. When I said it my voice was direct and straightforward and he knew I wasn't lying.

"No," I told him.

"Why are you here then?" There was defeat in his question.

Again, I told him truthfully, "I thought I knew where to look."

"That cave on Lorenzo Ponti's estate has been in use as a mushroom farm for over thirty years," Watson told me.

I felt Velda's knee twitch against mine, his words surprising the both of us. I didn't let my expression show what I felt, and asked, "How would you know that?"

"Because the area is inspected periodically. He has a healthy business there and the IRS keeps a close watch on those things. Nothing goes on there we don't know about."

"How big is it?"

He smiled indulgently and said, "The cave itself is about sixty feet wide and twenty tall. It goes back approximately one thousand feet. At the moment it is completely filled with a new mushroom crop. The place could hold many billion dollars, but be assured, there is nothing in there except fungi. Edible, of course."

"And the government agents are welcome on his estate?"

"They go through the proper notification. The process has been in place many years."

Velda and I looked at each other. There was no despair in our glances, just an air that had an "oh, well" attitude to it and Homer Watson took it all in.

"I'm sorry to spoil your expectations, Mr. Hammer. I'd much rather you did know and had told me. Frankly, though, I suspected this would happen. There is no way that a person like Dooley would have a part in a money movement like we are talking about."

"Probably not," I agreed.

"And now, where do you go from here?" he asked.

"To see the don, Homer."

His eyes narrowed again. "Why?"

"Because I'm looking for a killer, not a fortune."

Homer got up and picked up the tab on the corner of the table. I let him have it. It was like getting a rebate on my taxes.

When he left, Velda said, "About going to see Ponti . . ."

"I'm going in, kitten. You're staying on the outside near the phone. Every ten minutes I'm going to call . . ."

"I'll stay in the room."

"Good. When I get ready to come out I'll tell you, then give me thirty minutes to show up. If I don't, you call the state troopers right away. Not the local constabulary . . . the troopers. Then call Pat and get ready to raise hell on the Ponti estate."

"You think it might get that bad?"

"Anything can go sour when you're talking about billions."

"Mike . . ."

"What?"

"You have a gun on you?"

"No. I was bluffing poor old Homer."

"Ponti won't buy a bluff, Mike."

"I know. They'll frisk me anyway, so I'll go in without one."

I kept my lights on bright and leaned on the horn. I kept hitting it intermittently until a shotgun came in the open side window and both barrels banged against the side of my head. "What the hell do ya think you're doing?" the city-accented voice demanded.

"I want to see the don, that's what I want!" I could be just as demanding and it made the guy think, which wasn't easy for him to do.

"He ain't seeing nobody!"

"He'll be seeing me, buddy, and if you don't tell him I'm here he'll rip your tail off."

This time he was real confused. "Who you supposed to be?"

"Hammer, Mike Hammer. Now you get to the don and tell him I'm here."

No way was he going to see Ponti. He let out a yell for Sammy, and when his backup got there, he shouted, "This punk wants to see the don. What're we gonna do with him?"

Sammy looked in the window, stared a second and looked up at his partner. "You know who this dude is?"

"He said he was Hammer."

"Yeah, he's a damned PI. He's the one who knocked off Azi Ponti on the docks."

"Does the don know that?"

"Sure he knows it." Sammy reached in his pocket and

took out a walkie-talkie, touched the SEND button and told somebody what he had. A full minute went by and another city voice said to send him in. Sammy told me, "Go slow, leave your lights on and do what you're told."

The shotgun came away from my head reluctantly and when the pair backed off I put the gearshift in drive and eased on up the road. Every so often a flashlight would bathe the car, lingering on my face a few seconds. Finally I reached the last bend and there was the house awash in lights. The men came out of the dark beside me and escorted the car right up to the door. Four more stood there, guns in their hands. Ordinarily, I'd be flattered to see how they showed their respect, calling out all that firepower, but right now they were holding all the cards and I was going to play it cool, real cool.

I cut the motor, stuck the keys in my pocket and slid out the door. The first frisk was fast, to make sure I didn't have any big equipment to lay on them. The second time it was more detailed, looking for a knife or a hidden razor blade. When they were sure I was clean one waved me to the door, touched the bell and it opened. There was Patterson standing there with a small automatic in his fist and a nasty smile on his face. Had not the don come in at that moment something would have happened, but Ponti said, "Get in here, Hammer."

There were only the two of us in the room, but outside the closed doors there was the army. Somewhere eyes would be watching through concealed apertures to make sure everything stayed calm.

"Drink?" Ponti offered.

I didn't have any wine taster here, so I said, "Whatever you're having."

Don Ponti made two Canadian Club and ginger ale

highballs in tall glasses with plenty of ice, handed me one and indicated that I take a seat. It looked like a nice, friendly meeting, but both of us had felt guns grow hot in our hands and knew well enough how the system worked. I asked the don if I could use his phone and picked it up even before he nodded that I could. I dialed Velda's number, gave her the digits from the don's phone and hung up.

"She'll keep calling back," Ponti stated.

"Every ten minutes."

"I like that, but it's not necessary."

I shrugged and sipped my drink. "Why take chances?"

"You know, I could have used you in my family," he said.

"Don Ponti, I couldn't take all that excitement."

"You came in here alone."

"Did I?"

He didn't like my tone and frowned. When I grinned he lost the worry lines and smiled back. "By rights I should kill you, Mike. For killing my son I should kill you, even if Azi did a bad thing. I believe you when you said you wanted to warn me of the treachery on the docks, but I was prepared for such a thing. You think I would not know what a target I was, coming off the boat at night like that? You think that when the boss goes away everything stays the same. Someone takes his place for a little while, then gets so he feels like that place is where he really belongs."

"I appreciate your consideration, don," I said flatly.

"Certainly, I couldn't kill you until you tell me where the money is."

"Remember how it was in the old days, Don Ponti? You could take a guy and pull his fingernails out or cut his feet off . . . just about anything to make him talk and believe me, he'd talk. You think I could take that?"

Ponti snorted and sipped his drink. "No, you could *not* take that, Mike. You would talk. The trouble is, you would not have anything to say that I want to hear."

I looked at him over the top of my glass.

"Dooley told you, Mike, but you haven't figured it out yet. Am I right?"

"You got it."

"Then why are you here?"

"To find out who put a hit order on Dooley."

"Why do you worry about that man? He was a nothing. He was not *with* us, and now he's dead." For a moment he stared at the wall, then continued. "For me, it is not worth hating him now. I made a mistake. Because he was not one of us I trusted him. He had no taste for money at all. Many times I showed him how he could make a quick score, but he couldn't be bothered. That's why I trusted him. The heads of the other families went with my reasoning."

"You were going to store that money in that cave of yours, weren't you?"

"That was the original idea. It would go in the back section, then the cave would be closed off in a natural manner with a hidden entrance."

"And you'd keep the mushroom farm going to disguise the operation."

"You have done your homework, Mr. Hammer."

Hell, if Homer hadn't let it slip I never would have known about it at all. At least I didn't have to do a personal search of the place now. Ponti wasn't lying to me, but he wasn't letting me off the hook either. I looked at my watch, picked up the phone and called Velda again. I told her everything was cool and hung up.

"What about Dooley, Don Ponti . . . did he do something that put you wise to what he was doing?"

Ponti suddenly looked puzzled and a little bit sad. He lost that toughness that used to be a part of him, that constant wariness that kept him aware of every movement an enemy made. It wasn't so much that he lost it as that a degree of acceptance seemed to surround him. He wasn't a young guy anymore. He probably was in his early eighties and the last of a breed that came in on one generation and went out on another.

"I should have remembered not to trust anybody," he said. "These are times when nobody has a friend."

"Not in your line of work."

"Why would he do that to me? He should have known what would happen."

"Ponti," I said to him, "Dooley didn't do a *thing* to you. He didn't even steal your money. He just took it out of circulation and put it where *nobody* could get it. He finally got sick of what happened to the world. He fought a war to save it then watched it go to pot, helped on by the nudging of the crooks of the world. What he did was make a statement, but so far nobody has heard that statement. It's buried with that money."

While I was talking the toughness came back to his face. "It was too big a pile for anybody to hide for long. You know that, don't you?"

"Yeah, I know that."

"No buildings are available to warehouse it either."

"So?"

"The cave was the perfect answer. It would have worked." His lips parted in a tight smile. "I understand you and your secretary looked at the cave at Harris' place too."

"Nice spy system you have."

"What did you think about it?"

"Empty, what else? A great spot for a bootlegger. Hasn't got any bats either. How do you keep them out of your mushroom farm?"

"Could be the activity. Could be the cyanide they clean the beds with."

The conversation was going noplace, so out of the blue I asked Ponti, "How did you think you were going to get away with it?"

His shrug was eloquent. "While the transfer was being made, I was not a part of it. So far I've never been inside a prison. I don't want to go now. Had Dooley not screwed me, this would have been the move of the century." He suddenly gazed at me curiously. "Have you ever wondered why the government never tried to deport me?"

I didn't say a word. He knew the answer.

"I am a citizen. The day my mother got off the ship from Sicily I was born. She had me on a table on Ellis Island; I was given a birth certificate by a doctor who was inspecting all the immigrants. That is why I could not be deported."

"That's too bad, Lorenzo. Deportation could have saved your life."

"I think anybody who could be called my enemy is a long time dead. The new dons take, er, suggestions from me. It seems that they are short on experience. There is no more *commissione,* the way it was. I think you know . . . business goes on as usual. With the way the world is going, business will probably increase."

I felt my skin crawl at the calm way he said it.

"If this incredible amount of money just . . . disappears . . . how much will it bother you?"

He shrugged, a gently eloquent shrug you almost had to believe. "It would be a loss. Not something that couldn't be recouped, of course. This time it would be quicker to accumulate."

"What makes you think so?"

He said, "This world, Mr. Hammer. Look at it. Every city is full of violence, every country on the brink of war. The people are so wrapped up in troubles that they turn to anything we want to supply them with to keep their minds from unwinding. You know that. The government has to run its own sting operation to keep its members in line. The police and politicians go down the drain when corruption pays them ten times what their employers do. You read about it in the papers all the time. This is nothing new to you, is it?"

I shook my head. He was right on the mark.

"All this has just put me to a lot of trouble, that's all."

"Not everybody is going to think like that, Lorenzo. No matter what you say there's a lot of money somewhere. There are a lot of hotheads who will do anything to get at it. You're not dealing with great intelligences, and you damn well know that too. It was you and your kind that set this thing in motion and it's not going to just cool down and go back to business as usual."

"Mike," he said to me coldly, "you are the loose cannon in this affair. Dooley told you something that got you involved and you will be as much of a target as me. But you don't own an army to cover your back like I do."

For a moment I didn't answer him, then said, "Nobody can get to you, don?"

He liked the way I used his title and smiled indulgently. "No," he told me. "You can see how careful I am. My men are well taken care of. That business at the docks should have shown you that."

"Who instigated it, Don Ponti?"

A sense of sad annoyance crossed his face. "It does not

matter now, Mr. Hammer. Death eliminates many enemies. It also takes a lot of talent out of circulation. Sometimes you lose somebody close to you, but that is business, the business of life. It cannot be mourned as if it is the end of all things."

The years had bored into the don deeper than I had thought. They had dried up the incredible reservoir of controlled rage that could direct violence to achieve his own ends. At one time nothing would have shown in his mannerisms, no emotional expression would have crossed his face. His eyes could tell you that you were going to die easy or hard, sooner or later. They could tell you that you were going to die now too. One look at his guys could have your business burned or your family wiped out. Anything to bring you into submission.

Right now his eyes just had a hard, used look. They weren't too sure anymore.

I said, "What do you want from me, Lorenzo?"

Those eyes of his drilled right into me again. They were still hard, but the steel wasn't there any longer.

"Right now you're just useless, Hammer. If you really knew anything you would have been right on top of it. I think you know what I'm going to do. You're going to be covered by pros of my own. Anything you come up with, they'll know about."

"Your guys are garbage heads, Don Ponti."

"I didn't say 'my guys' Hammer. I said, 'pros of my own.' You should know what money can buy."

There are times when the talking has stopped and you get out while you still have a chance. This was one of them. I made a phone call to Velda. I didn't even say so long. I just nodded to Don Lorenzo Ponti and got up. He followed me to the door, opened it and did something with his eyes to the guys standing there. Whatever passed between them was understood and they just watched while I got into my car.

One of them made a mistake and I heard a pump automatic shotgun jack a shell into the chamber.

There was a turnaround area designed to fit one radius of a normal vehicle and I swung into it gently. I had made almost the full circle that led to the single road back to civilization when my headlights picked up the almost imperceptible shift of their shoulders and I knew that the don had changed his mind. I was more of a threat than he had assumed. He was still that deadly animal from the old days, eaten up with the white heat of hate, fed by the craving of ambition, and I was going out in one great broadside of armament right into the driver's door and window and I'd wind up being compressed right inside my car to a bale-sized piece of metal destined for the smelters of some foreign country.

But I hit the gas pedal and twisted the wheel so that I went right into that group of killers and saw Patterson fly off the hood and the one with the shotgun let a blast off into the night sky that was almost as loud as his shriek and out of the corner of my eyes saw the big door slam behind the don as my wheels went over something that cursed and yelled, then I cranked the wheel back, picked up the ruts in the driveway and headed out.

Luckily, I saw the lights through the trees, cut my own, and pulled to one side where the brush shielded me. The big car that was roaring up toward the house never stopped because the driver never saw me, and as soon as he was past I got out into the cleared area and drove back to the highway. There should have been more of the don's men along the way, but whoever drove that big car must have picked them up.

It was a new scene now. There wouldn't be any more

peaceful days, or empty time to plan the next move. As far as Ponti was concerned, I wasn't somebody to follow, but a mad dog to be hunted and shot dead, any way, any how, and the sooner the better.

10

I GOT BACK TO THE MOTEL in time to catch Velda tossing our gear into her rental car and slid to a stop beside her. The sharp lines of anxiety on her face turned to instant joy and she dropped a piece of luggage and threw her arms around my neck before I was all the way out of the car.

Pulling her off me wasn't easy. "What's going on, kitten? You all right?"

"Oh, Mike, yes, I'm all right. But you didn't call on time like you said you would and I phoned the state troopers. They should be at Ponti's place right now!" She read my eyes and felt my fingers tighten on her arms. "What happened?"

I told her.

"Did you kill anybody?"

"I didn't stay around to look, but I'll tell you this: I tried to get as many as I could. They were going to gun me down. You call Pat?"

"Yes. He was going to get the troopers up here on the phone. This is a *no publicity* deal and he's got Homer Watson to back him up." She paused, squinted at me and added, "Will that do any good?"

"Maybe. We're not in Pat's jurisdiction, but Homer has that federal edge."

"Now what?"

"We move. We need a safer place than this. I don't even want Homer tracking us down. Tomorrow we take your car back and we stick with mine. There must be a half million other Ford sedans like this out on the road so it won't be easily noticed."

"Just get it washed and nobody will know it's yours," she told me.

A sleepy night clerk checked us out and went back to bed. It took a half hour to locate a raunchy little motel complex whose *Vacancy* light was still on. Another sleepy guy got off his couch to let me sign in, took my money in advance and handed me a key. On the way out I saw him flip the vacancy light off even though only three other cars were parked outside the rooms.

I backed up to the door in case we needed a fast getaway. We only took in what we were going to need, pulled the curtains shut and turned on the bathroom light with the door partially closed to leave only a soft glow. In the thirty minutes between motels I had made pretty sure nobody had been on our tail. Traffic was almost at zero and I had made a one-eighty-degree turn after I passed the motel, approaching it from a different direction in case I did have a tail. For five minutes I had sat in the dark, lights off, outside the office building, waiting and watching. When I was sure I was clear, I went inside.

We both cleaned up, then got fully dressed except for our shoes, finally easing back into the twin beds. If anything happened and we did have to make a fast move, we'd be ready for it.

Velda said softly, "I feel like a fireman waiting for the alarm to go off."

"Quiet," I told her.

"Don't I get a kiss good night?"

I held back a laugh and slid out of bed. There was enough light so I could see her eyes glisten. "Just a plain old kiss, doll. Nothing fancy, hear?"

"Are you talking about me or you?" she teased.

I kissed her. It wasn't a plain old good night kiss at all. It almost erupted into something else, but I pushed her away and got back in my own bed. In the darkness I heard her chuckle.

The TV news out of Albany ran the story of the blood-letting on Don Lorenzo Ponti's country estate. There were four seriously injured New York hoodlums transported to the local hospital. None were dead, but their injuries were critical.

Inside the main house, the body of the head of the New York Mafia family lay slumped on the floor, shot dead by three bullets to the back of the head, a typical gangland type of elimination. The only thing wrong was that one too many slugs were fired. The caliber of the bullets wasn't announced, but from the general description of the body damage, it wasn't done with high-powered .22's.

Across the room was the body of Leonard Patterson with a broken leg and severe upper torso injuries, but the cause of death was from a .38 automatic still in the dead hand of the don. No other persons were on the estate when the police arrived. Interrogations would take place when the medical authorities allowed it, probably in several days.

Finally, the stuff had hit the fan.

There was a breakdown of what had happened, and according to the reporter there was an impending fight between Patterson and Ponti, but the don had shot before Patterson could get his own gun out of his belt. The third party who had killed the don was not identified, but there were fresh tire tracks around the building that could be identified and plaster casts were being made by the police. The state troopers had been alerted to the situation by a phone call from an unidentified woman. Since their response other police agencies had been brought to the scene to continue the investigation.

Velda asked, "How long do we have before they latch on to us?"

"When they dust that room, my prints will be there," I said. "I left some identifiable tire tracks in the soft ground, that's for sure, so that will put me right on top of things. There's no telling what those slobs that I ran down will say. Maybe they'll talk, maybe not."

"Times are tough, huh?" I looked at her. She didn't even sound worried.

"One thing is, I didn't ice Ponti or Patterson. Whoever was in that car that roared up while I was on the way out is the logical suspect."

"Have you got any good guesses?"

I went over and turned the channels on TV. Nothing like this had hit the area since prohibition so every station was carrying a report of the situation. A couple were even playing a local angle of having the residents keep a lookout for new faces in the area and calling in any odd occurrences they may have noticed.

"This isn't local," I said disgustedly. "They're dealing with a damned rich organization that can buy anything it wants."

"Except it's not so big right now, is it, Mike?"

"Right," I agreed. "It's money that makes this old world go around, so we're back to the eighty-nine billion bucks again. You know . . . there are a lot of countries that could run a credible war with that kind of funding."

"And that leaves us with a problem, doesn't it?"

"Like what?"

"Like where do we go from here?"

The TV was too loud, so I turned it off. I wiped my hand across my face, but everything stayed blurred.

"Want a new thought?" Velda asked me.

"Damn right."

"Let's get married. At least then I could never testify against you."

"I didn't do anything to testify against, doll."

"We stayed together in a motel room."

"Nothing happened."

"A jury would never believe that," she said.

"Doesn't matter," I told her. "We didn't cross any state lines."

I got that pensive look again, so I mussed up her hair, my fingers running through the long silkiness of it. I could almost close my eyes and feel the color of it. I let my fingertips run down her neck, massaging her gently, and she turned her head with her eyes closed and if she had been a cat she would have purred. Then I felt the color of her hair again and you can't feel color. You have to see it. But I felt it.

I said, "Come on, let's not waste time."

Morning traffic was light and we took our place in the stream of workers heading for the New York Thruway. Once we turned onto it we were buried amidst the semi-trailers and general commuters heading south.

At the Albany off-ramp I swung right, aiming for a mid-city building I had been to before. Parking was still available and I grabbed a spot and shut the engine off. Velda hadn't said a word for the past half hour, letting her eyes scan the sides of the roads for police cars. Now she looked at the building I had parked near and got out when I did, a strange expression tightening her face.

Without saying a word, I hooked my hand under her arm and led her toward those big, official-looking doors where well-dressed, determined-looking people were going in. Just as we reached them two uniformed cops came out, barely glanced at us and kept on going. Anybody going into the courthouse didn't seem suspicious.

Except for Velda. She didn't know what was going on until we reached the proper door where marriage licenses were issued, then her hand squeezed my arm so tightly I was glad she didn't have it on my neck. We were the only ones in the room where we got our instructions on the blood testing and the address of the nearest facility to do the job, took the booklet on the counter that discussed the solemnity and requirements of a good marriage, thanked the clerk and told her we'd be back.

As far as Velda was concerned, the deed was almost as good as done. We would probably have to wait a few days for the blood tests to be completed, but somehow she was going to make sure that situation was expedited to its utmost. An hour later we had gone through the ritual, then she spent fifteen minutes talking to someone in the doctor's office. When she came out she was all smiles, a satisfied look spread across that beautiful face like a kid who had just pulled off a successful raid on the cookie jar.

"It will be ready at four-thirty," she announced. You'd think she had just won the Super Bowl single-handed. "The license bureau closes at five. Now can we eat lunch?"

Time wasn't measured by a watch anymore. The gentle

burning of the hole in my side told me that I had slipped up on the medication schedule again. I took my pills with my Danish pastry while Velda dug into a big plate of bacon and eggs. Several times she glanced at me nervously, knowing what was happening, and once asked if I were all right.

"Just the usual," I explained. "Ralph Morgan tried to tell me, but I keep forgetting. It just isn't easy to stay relaxed. Not in this business, anyway. But I'm not dying, so stay cool, kitten."

When we finished the waitress poured us another cup of coffee and we sat back sort of grinning at each other, wondering what being married was going to be like. Hell, we were together most of the time, in wild situations where your life depended on your partner, what else could be new when you were married?

She broke off our eye contact and rummaged in her handbag, bringing out a white envelope. "I forgot to show you these. There was a one-hour developing place near the motel and I had them done."

What she gave me were photos of Slipped Disk Harris' cave area, and although the focus was fine and the scene well lit, the subject matter was arranged in a pretty amateur way. I flipped through them, noting again how that great area could well have housed many thousands of bottles of booze. In the floor markings were the outlines of pallets, and the grooves made by the wheels of the trucks that had delivered the booze to the customers in the big cities.

I was studying the one where the ceiling had come down when she said, "No sign of bats?"

"No bats," I reiterated. I took another sip of coffee and knew I was frowning.

"What are you thinking, Mike?"

"You got a card from McClain and Leeds Surveying, didn't you?"

"Uh-huh." She went into her handbag again and came out with the card.

I checked the address and handed it back. "Come on kitten. We have things to do."

She was going to make a good wife, all right. There were no questions. I paid the bill and we got in the car. Thirty minutes later I pulled up in front of the survey building, parked and went inside. Johnny Leeds said hello with a big handshake and another one of those glances toward Velda that I'd have to get used to seeing.

"Well, did you see the Harris place?" he asked.

I grinned at him and nodded. "Yeah, and it's a great spot."

"You must be kidding!"

"No way, Johnny."

"But I told you it was a depressed area." He watched me a moment, then he got it. "You really are talking about raising a family, aren't you?"

"Let's start off by saying a vacation spot might be more in line. Those old buildings can be demolished pretty easily and you sure can't beat the scenic value of that spot. If the worst comes to the worst, I can raise mushrooms in that cave up there."

"Sure you can," he replied jokingly. "What's your problem with the place?"

"No problem. I need information. There's a caretaker there of sorts and I'd like to find out how long he's been there and who was there before him. I want to locate the owner and see if the place is on the market. Can you handle that?"

"Easy. If you want to buy, do you want me to recommend an agency?"

"You bet. Just make sure you get a cut of the sale."

"You bet," he replied with a wink. "Incidentally, did you hear about the killings up at the Ponti estate? That's not too far from the Harris place."

"Heard it on the morning news. Don't suppose they'll be missed, though. They know who did it?"

"If they do they're not saying yet. A dragnet is out for somebody."

"Well, at least we know old Harris is well tucked into bed," I said. "When do you want me to check back with you?"

"Late this afternoon. That be all right?"

"Just fine. See you then. If I get tied up, I'll call."

"One more thing. These real estate agents will want to know about financing and—"

"It'll be cash on the barrelhead, Johnny. No banks, no mortgages."

"Way to go," he said, and waved me into the car.

As we pulled away from the curb, Velda mused, "No banks, no mortgages . . ."

"What's wrong with that?"

"You're talking like a damn millionaire about to buy the place."

"It's a great idea."

"Where would you get the money?"

"Oh, I'll dig it up."

"Like they'll dig up Hoffa's body?"

"Something like that."

There was a pregnant pause, and she said, "Do I have anything to say about this?"

"No."

"When we're married . . ."

"You're not married yet, kitten."

Her voice sounded tiny and defeated, just a little, "Oh."

So I reassured her. "I'm not saying it's a bad idea, doll. I just said we're not married *yet.*"

The satisfied grin she gave me made me feel a lot better.

I turned on the radio and punched the buttons for the local Albany station. The big news was still the Ponti murder. What they hadn't figured out yet was the damage done by an unidentified car that had banged around a bunch of bad guys. Nobody was talking yet and there was no broken glass or shards of evidence to identify the make or model of the car. The paint samples indicated that the car was black. Later, laboratory analysis would point out the maker and, most likely, the model and year of my vehicle. Which didn't bother me. Ford had manufactured a million of them.

Twenty minutes later I spotted the thruway up ahead, pulled into the left lane and turned onto the on-ramp heading north. Velda's head jerked around, surprised. "Where are we going, Mike?"

"Back to Harris' place."

"Mike . . . that place will be filled with cops!"

"Why? Nobody was killed there. We didn't leave any tracks leading to his place."

"They can have roadblocks up around there."

"Not on the thruway, kitten, and if they had any at all, they're probably down by now. Roadblocks only last for so long. If they haven't caught the killer by now, it won't happen in a roadblock."

I gassed up right off the thruway, and when Velda went to the ladies' room I reached down under the seat and brought out my .45, still wrapped in its leather shoulder holster. I slipped off my jacket, climbed into the speed rig, tying it in place and fastening it to my belt. I jacked a shell into the chamber, thumbed the hammer back to half cock and slipped the safety on. When my jacket was back on I felt normal again. I had been too long without that weapon. For too many years it had been a close companion and saying hello to it again was like shaking hands with an old friend.

After five minutes Velda came back. She was looking away from the office section, not wanting anybody to be able to describe her. I had done the same thing, but a little bit differently, when I paid the bill.

The county road I was looking for wasn't far away and I picked it up, drove to the familiar spot where it led to Slipped Disk Harris' old quarters, and slowed down right after I made the turn.

Velda said, "What's the matter?"

"Remember Slateman telling us he spotted the car a mile away?"

"So?"

"Harris probably cut a see-through opening in the trees for that purpose."

"What difference does that make? Harris is long dead."

"I don't like gimmicks, kitten."

"Are we going to walk?"

"No . . . but you keep looking off to your right and if you start to see any of the buildings up there, tell me. I'll keep the other side covered."

We hadn't gone an eighth of a mile when she held out her hand and said, "Stop!" I hit the brakes quickly then, keeping the engine running, got out of the car and walked around the front of it. Velda had spotted it just in time. Running straight as an arrow up the side of the mountain was a path through the tree line. The brush was grown up head high, but the line of sight was perfect. Anybody up there could spot movement down on the road below. A car driving past would never notice that strip of emptiness and a beautiful ambush would be waiting for him above. Unless they had a prearranged signal set up. But that was long ago. Those devices wouldn't be in use now, but nature hadn't closed off the visual sighting slash in the trees yet.

Very slowly I drove past the opening. It would be movement that attracted the eye and at my pace nobody was going to notice. We passed the wreckage of the old chain-drive Mack truck, followed the ruts in the road very carefully and finally came out on the edge of the estate.

When I stopped again, Velda said, "Now what's wrong?"

"You feel anything?" I asked her.

"Clue me in."

"Slateman."

"He didn't know we were coming."

"There's a wood-burning cookstove in his kitchen. No smoke."

"He's not cooking."

"Look, he doesn't start a fire for every meal."

"If a fire burns down, will it smoke?"

I shook my head. "Not necessarily, but chimney heat always leaves a disturbance in the air."

Softly, Velda said, "Mike, New York people aren't supposed to know these things."

"New York people who were army personnel sneaking up on country places the enemy occupied did."

We sat there for five minutes, then I put the gearshift into drive again and touched the gas pedal. Nothing happened. We got up to the door of Slateman's house and stopped. Still, nothing happened. The only sounds were those of the wind whistling through the trees. Over to the west was a rumble of faraway thunder.

I got out of the car and made Velda walk behind me. It wasn't the best way to approach a place you weren't sure of, but I was beginning to think it was the memory of what this area was, the business that held it together, that gave me that spooky feeling. There was still something left in the old wood and fieldstone that seemed to radiate trouble.

The door was latched, the fire was out and the place was empty. There were no dirty dishes, the garbage can was empty and everything seemed to be right in place. There was just an uncanny feeling of *aloneness* that shouldn't be there.

Velda had taken it all in too. Finally she said, "He'd have to go to town sooner or later, Mike. He wouldn't leave the stove going then and he would have cleaned up beforehand."

"That's a long walk, kid."

"He'd have some way to get to town. He wasn't that much of a recluse."

I nodded in agreement. "Guess you're right, but it doesn't hurt to be careful. Come on, let's go see the cave."

"What are we looking for?"

"If I told you, you'd think I was crazy."

Slateman had left his heavy-duty flashlight right on the table. I took that and gave Velda the one out of the car. She hefted it, thinking it more of a club than a light. When she was satisfied, we moved out across the field.

Finding the entrance was easy this time. Velda balked a moment until I said, "No bats, remember?"

She took a deep breath and walked in behind me. We kept the lights moving, covering the area as best we could, but nothing had changed since the last time. We followed the wall, stepping over the junk on the floor, kicking away things that made small tingling sounds and avoiding the broken remnants of whiskey bottles that had been sampled, drained and dropped by workers getting a few perks in for their labors.

Three-quarters of the way around we came to the place I had wanted to see. It was the rubble from the roof that had come crashing down many years ago and had been pushed against the back wall out of the way. I ran the light up at the ceiling and saw some scars in the stone, then lowered it to cover the angled pile to my left. Dirt and dust were thick on everything. I crouched down, picked up a handful and let it sift through my fingers.

Odd, I thought. Dust wasn't dusty after all. It had an abrasiveness like fine sand.

Velda's light hit me right in the eyes.

When she realized the light was blinding me she pulled it down to the ground and said, "What are you looking for, Mike?"

I was just about to answer her when another voice said, "Yeah, Mike, tell her what you were looking for."

There was the faintest metallic click and I knew the hammer had gone back on a gun.

Velda sucked her breath in with an audible gasp.

The voice in the darkness behind us wasn't coming from Slateman. It was young and hard, the kind that had death right behind it and wouldn't wait very long at all to spring into a killing frenzy.

I said, "It's about time you got here, Ugo."

My tone slowed him down an instant. Ugo Ponti wasn't a fast thinker.

"Why do you suppose that, Hammer?"

"You had the numbers, didn't you?"

"Sure I did. I'm not so damn dumb. That kid put me right on them."

There was one thing I had to know. "Did you kill the slob, Ugo?"

"I would have, just like I shot his old man, but a hundred bucks bought his story and I didn't have any cops chasing me."

"They'll be chasing you now, Ugo."

"What makes you think so?"

"Because your father is dead, that's why. You knocked off your own father, didn't you?"

There was no remorse in his voice. He seemed to be almost proud of what he had done. "My old man lost his guts. All those Mustache Petes tried to keep everything the way it was and it doesn't go that way. Those bastards grabbed everything that should have come to us and got what they deserved."

My legs were starting to cramp up, but I had to keep him talking. "And now you're in a big empty cave, Ugo."

"Yeah, but I got you and your woman here and you know where the stuff is."

"You don't see it, do you? What makes you think I can get to it?"

"Don't give me that crap, Hammer. Your buddy Dooley told you. No big deal. He just told you and you're here to do it."

Velda's light was still pointing at the floor. The both of us were in the glow of our own flashlights and Ugo was in total darkness. Any movement either one of us made would lay us out. There was no telling by that click I had heard whether he had a small arm or a shotgun, but if it were a shotgun, he could get us both with the first blast.

Without asking, I uncrouched from the floor very slowly, leaving my flashlight on the ground, my mind racing, trying to line up the best odds.

Ugo said, "That's right, Mike. Nice and easy. Now, once more, what were you looking for?"

Now, if Velda would only get the drift of my thoughts. It had to happen all at once and happen right or we were both dead. There was no way I could flash a sign to her, so she had to work on reflexes alone, and that strange state of mind that can exist between partners who have been together so long they act in total unison.

I said, "I'm not looking, Ugo. I already found it."

And as I kicked off the light on the ground she flipped her switch and we both hit the dirt as Ugo pumped four shotgun rounds in our direction before he knew he hadn't hit either of us. But by then I had the .45 out, the safety off and the hammer back and I aimed right where I had last seen the muzzle flash and let the deafening roar of the old Colt automatic thunder in the cave. The single bullet smashed into something that clattered, but didn't kill, and when I flashed the light on it caught Ugo Ponti, the new don, heir to Lorenzo's throne and domain, scrabbling in the dirt for the mangled shotgun my slug had smashed into useless junk, and when he saw what it was like, let out a wild scream and raised the shotgun like a shield. I triggered the .45 again and the slug smashed into the metal breech of his weapon that crashed into his chin and he went down with his eyes bugging out and his breathing hoarse with pain.

I walked up to the slob and let the light wash over him. Blood ran down from the cut on his chin and his body made a few involuntary jerks before realization was in his eyes. He didn't know what was coming next, but the hatred that oozed from his pupils was filled with a violent venom that nothing could diminish. They finally dropped to the gun in my hand, and when I started to raise it his lips drew back with the fierceness of his crazy desire to kill me one way or another but knowing that once I had him looking down that big bore of the .45 it was going to be the last thing he would see.

Then the big lights came on. One after another as nine of them came pouring into the cave. There were four uniformed police officers and another four in plainclothes. The ninth was covered with grime and seemed mad enough to spit. I said, "Hello, Homer."

He didn't answer me. He said, "What the hell have you done?"

"Caught you a killer, friend." I nudged Ugo with my toe. "He's not dead. He's all smashed up inside and if you don't get him to a hospital he sure as heck will kick it. But he'll remember all this, and he'll talk. He's the one who wasted Dooley and killed his own father."

"You can prove this, I suppose," Homer said sarcastically.

Velda handed him her Sony recorder. "Here's a tape of him admitting it, Homer. Someplace you'll locate his .357, then you'll have him on all charges."

Homer took the Sony and touched the button and listened to it, then rolled the tape back and let it play. He caught all the action and I grinned like an ape because Velda had caught on just the way I had hoped. She told him, "He couldn't see me move my finger. I just flipped the button to RECORD and got the whole thing. I figured that if he killed us there would be something left to show for our efforts."

"You're up the creek on me, though," I told Homer.

"You think so?"

"Absolutely. I'm licensed in New York State, I've disabled a killer without killing him, so now what?"

"Where's the money, Hammer?"

"You don't see any, do you?"

"If it weren't here, none of us would be here," he said.

"Well, why don't you call in all your specialists and search this place. If you find anything, it's all yours or

Uncle Sam's. And while you're at it, look for the nice little old man who used to live here. I have an idea that Ugo got here in time to erase him, too. There's plenty of places to hide a body on this mountain, but a few dogs or some locals ought to be enough to find out where Ugo put Slateman."

It was happening again. The tension had hit a new high and my body felt all the pressure in one point. It was as if an animal was gnawing a hole into me, a subtle pain like a great spiderweb radiating out from the wound. I walked over to Velda, and when I put my hand on her she knew it wasn't a gesture, but me holding on to keep from doubling over. I still had the .45 in my hand and she took it away and slipped it into the holster under my coat.

Homer kept watching me, not knowing just what to say. So I said it. "You want me for anything, Mr. Watson?"

"Where are you going to be?"

"Don't worry. I'll stay in touch," I said. I kept my arm around Velda and she put hers around me, not touching the hole in my side. The uniformed cops and the ones in suits didn't know what to make of the whole matter, but since Homer didn't try to stop us, they let us pass, keeping our path lit as we did.

Velda said, "Are you all right?"

I shook my head.

When we reached the car she opened the passenger door and let me slide in, then she got behind the wheel. Her eyes asked where we were going and I said, "Get the . . . blood test results. Then go . . . to the courthouse. We can just make it . . . if you kick it hard."

She made one other stop. I tried to talk her out of it, but she pulled into a Texaco station, grabbed a packet of crackers and handed them to me in the car. I got my pills down, but not quite in time. The pain grew with a terrible intensity before it finally slackened off just before we reached Albany.

The clinic was right on the way and we picked up the blood test results. Neither one of us had any dirty diseases. We made it to the clerk at the courthouse too, just minutes before she was about to close her doors. We got the license to marry, paid the fee and went back outside.

It had been a long time since I had seen her so happy.

A sour taste had come up in my throat and my breathing became strained. Velda kept looking at me from the corner of her eye, then put her palm on my forehead and said, "Damn, you have a fever."

I closed my eyes and knew when the car stopped. It rolled again and my door opened and I knew it was Velda who was half carrying me into an air-conditioned room, laying me on a cushioning mattress. I felt her hands on me without knowing what they were doing because my mind was off in a crazy dream world that was nice because there was no pain in it.

There were voices. There were always voices. There were familiar voices and some that were harsh and almost threatening. But Velda's voice was always there and carried the real weight of authority and after a while all the other voices went away.

I woke up hungry, trying to remember something, but pain as an experience wasn't easy to bring back to mind. There was a soberness in my side and taking too deep a breath made it hurt again. When I moved my arm Velda was there like a shot, her hand finding mine. Then Ralph Morgan moved her hand away and felt for my pulse. When a half minute passed he nodded in a satisfied manner. I was still alive.

He asked me, "How do you feel, hero?"

"Like crap. But hungry. What day is this?"

"Friday."

"What date?"

He told me. No wonder I was hungry. I had been out of it four days. "What have you been feeding me?" I wanted to know.

"You wouldn't like to know, but you got it through tubes. Now stay quiet and we'll get something solid into you. Not much or you'd vomit it out."

"Vomit," I said disgustedly. "What a word to use before I eat."

Morgan let out a grunt and checked my side. The bandage appeared to be fresh and I was glad he didn't have to mess with it right then. Velda had gone to make me a breakfast as soon as I had come around. Now I looked at the tray she set down beside me. There was a single, soft-boiled egg in a cup next to a bowl of warm milk where a piece of buttered toast, well sugared, floated with simple elegance.

There are times when complaints don't do a bit of good. I let Velda spoon most of the egg into me, had half the toast and a few spoonfuls of warm milk, then I turned my head away. It was all I could eat. I let my eyes close and went back to sleep. I didn't need any pills now. The good doctor had been slipping the painkillers into my arm.

I didn't count the times I awoke and was fed. Each time I felt a little stronger and a little hungrier. There were times when voices came through the fog very clearly, but my mind refused to recognize them. I knew when the bandages came off and I was washed and dressed, and I felt Velda's hands shaving me. She had just finished cutting my hair when my eyes came open all the way and I knew I had gotten out of the black alley again.

Ralph Morgan was waiting with a big smile. Out of habit he felt my pulse again and asked, "How do you feel?"

"Not up to running any foot races," I told him. "What happened to me?"

"Stress, Sheer stress. You keep playing the game like you're twenty-five, Mike, but those days are long gone. You had one hell of a wound and you wouldn't listen to me. You didn't have to take a direct injury to that same spot to go down like a log. Heavy stress could do the same thing." He shook his head at me like I was a little kid. "And right in the middle of all this trouble you try to get married."

"Try?" Velda's voice sounded lame.

"The word itself implies failure," Morgan explained to her. "You *try* to jump over the obstacle means you didn't make it. You either do it or you don't. Just trying doesn't count."

I said, "That's stressful talk, doctor." I glanced at Velda and winked.

She winked back.

Another day passed before I got out of the bed. I was shaky as a newborn colt for a half hour, but after a shower I got dressed and made it around the room by myself. Nobody had to tell me that this was a waiting period. Velda and Morgan were making sure I was all right before they laid something else on me. So I had another cup of hot coffee, finished it slowly, then said, "Okay, what happens next?"

The courthouse had a conference room that could hold twenty people and it was filled completely. I had been introduced to all the bureau personnel but forgot their names as fast as I heard them. The only ones who mattered were Homer Watson and the governmental heavyweight who sat beside him at the head of the table.

No preliminaries were necessary here. Nobody read me

my rights, but I didn't expect them to. It wasn't that kind of interrogation. The head man's name was Austin Banger and twice he had been a senator from his home state. The papers called him the watchdog of the American economy and he had enough clout to rip the guts out of some lousy governmental programs and twice flipped industrial giants into prison for fleecing the public. Nobody liked him at all. The good guys despised him; the bad guys hated him.

Now he aimed right at my head.

"Mr. Hammer, do you know why you are here?"

Stress I knew all about. I said, "Tell me, Mr. Banger."

He sensed the odd tone in my voice and picked up the challenge. He made a movement in his chair and all his chairman-of-the-board instincts showed. His hands were flat on the table and the glint in his eyes was almost artificial. "Do you know how simple it would be to have us put you in prison for twenty years?"

I said one word to him and his face grew red.

This time he leaned forward, and although I was ten feet away it was like having his face right in mine. "Don't play games with me, Mr. Hammer."

"Then say what you have to say. I haven't got time for conversation."

Homer took him off the hook. The money mouse knew the score better than he did. "Mike . . . we had teams of experts in that cave on Harris' property. It was empty."

"I could have told you that."

"Ugo Ponti told us about the trail your friend Dooley left."

"It was a blind trail, Homer."

"What's that supposed to mean?"

"Dooley was making suckers of you."

"But you were his friend, Mr. Hammer. Were you made a sucker too?"

"No . . . I was just a tool to make sure you were really suckered. Dooley got you really entangled in one hell of a wild-goose chase. He was a nothing guy who didn't like the way the world treated him and decided to play a joke on it."

"Those billions of dollars were real!" He sounded as if I had them in my pocket.

"Don't be an idiot. You think the mobs would let that kind of loot get away from them?"

"If Lorenzo Ponti hadn't gotten killed . . ."

"But he's dead, Homer," I reminded him. "All of the families are very much in business. They still have their storefront headquarters around the cities. They still control the rackets and make deals with the narcotics cartels around the world. Their money will keep piling up, and although the tax men may tap into it once in a while, the big bulk will be free and clear in the strange places the families want to put it."

"Whose side are you on, Hammer?" Austin Banger broke in.

"Don't be a jerk. I'm only one guy. What good would it do to take sides?"

They all sat there like puppets. I didn't scare at all. Hell, I wasn't even stressed out. They had tried, but it didn't work. I got up from my chair and just to be a little snotty I opened my coat and hitched up my pants so they could catch a glimpse of the empty .45 holster. The real piece was out in the car but I made a statement. Not that it would have mattered. This was New York State, not Washington. The money mice all looked confused. It probably was the shortest meeting they had ever been to.

11

THE DOGS HAD FOUND SLATEMAN. His body had been dumped in an old stone-lined cistern not far from thc main house. The weathered wood cover had been dragged back over the hole and loose dirt and rock had been piled on top of it. There was a huge contusion on the side of his head and blood matted his face. His body was hung up on an old oil drum that floated down there too.

It was a good safe place to hide a body if nobody was going to look for it. Especially dogs. And it would be much better if the body were dead.

Slateman never reached that point. The club that Ugo Ponti had laid on him had almost but not quite killed him. There was a hairline fracture of his skull but the prognosis was good. He could still live out his years.

There wouldn't be much use for a commercial outfit to go in to demolish Harris' old buildings. The power of big government had gone to work and ripped everything apart looking for any kind of clue to those billions of dollars. Any standing structure had been flattened, every rock pried loose and inspected, the grounds were raked clean and gone over with metal detectors, and for all that work all they got was a trash pile of rusted cans, old chains from Mack trucks and a nice pile of assorted debris.

A fortune had been spent in looking.

A fortune they didn't find.

But did they ever try, and that was a nice word: *try*. It meant they failed.

They let Velda and me visit Slateman in the Albany hospital. He looked pretty small and pitiful, lying there in the bed. His head was bandaged and there was a swelling on one side of his jaw, but his mouth smiled when he saw us and he croaked out a weak hello.

I said, "The doctor told me you're going to be on your feet before long. You were pretty lucky, you know that?"

"Hell, I'm tough," he mumbled.

"How did he get to you?" Velda asked him.

"Snuck up on me, he did. I was getting ready to go down the road and hitch a ride to town." He took a deep breath before going on. "Then, blam, there he was. Didn't even say hello. Just swung something at my head and that's all I knew."

"You recognize him, Slateman?"

His head bobbed an affirmative. "Those cops . . . they had a picture. It was him, all right. You know who he was?"

"Yeah, we know."

"What happened to him?"

"Right now he's in the county jail medical facility here in Albany with the police guarding him every minute." I gave him a big grin. "Don't worry about him anymore.

He's got murder one charges going against him now. He is going to fall."

"Good," Slateman wheezed.

"What are you going to do?" I asked him.

"Y'mean after Medicare stops takin' care of me?"

I nodded.

"Sure beats me," he said. "I saw on TV where they wrecked my house and everything else."

"If somebody built a place up there would you like to take care of it?"

"Now, who'd do that?"

"Wait until you're on your feet, old-timer. We'll talk again, okay?"

"Sure thing."

We shook hands and left. I could feel his eyes on my back until we got in the elevator.

On the way down, Velda said, "Are you getting the jitters, Mike?"

"We have the blood tests, we have the license, now all we have to find is someone to tie the knot."

She paused and squeezed my arm. "You going to fink out on me?"

"I'm thinking about it, so stop bugging me."

"Mike . . ."

"Not long ago you told me to finish this thing. Remember?"

She didn't get annoyed because I jostled her memory. She suddenly became my business partner again and realized that the job came first and there was no way to talk me out of it.

Her smile came slowly. It wasn't grim. It said she understood and was ready to go along with my decision. "Okay, boss," she said.

You can't just leave things like that. I looked at that

beautiful face and wondered how Hollywood hadn't picked up on it years ago. She was dressed the way a business executive should be dressed, but there was that way clothes filled and swerved around unmistakable bodily outlines that couldn't be concealed and I realized why the clients and the CEO's in the restaurants and the college kids on the street looked at me the way they did.

I said, "Come with me, kid, and I'll get you some candy."

Velda stayed in the car around the corner from the store I went into. The manager gave me the big smile he saved for men getting ready to enter into the state of matrimony, though how he could tell his customers' intentions was beyond me.

I said, "I want a two-carat diamond, emerald cut, set in gold. I want top quality, and when you show it to me, I want your loupe so I can check the stone myself. I'll pay by check and I have plenty of identification. Can you handle that?"

His smile never faded. He nodded and went behind the counter. I could see what was on display, but he didn't pick one from the case. What he showed me came from a small rack, separately locked, beneath my line of vision. His fingers flipped open the small box and nested in a black velvet bed was the engagement ring. He handed me the loupe, watched as I inspected the quality of the gem, and when I put it back in its container I said, "Very nice."

"It's very expensive," he told me.

"About fifteen thousand, I'd say."

"Quite right. Actually, you're five hundred under the asking price, but given the circumstances, fifteen will do it."

If you're going to play the game, you might as well enjoy it. After this check I'd have about two thousand left in the office account, but the bills were all paid and there still was another week to refurbish my economic future.

I dug out my driver's license and handed it to him with the check. He took down my license number after ascertaining that I matched the photo in the plastic and handed me the box his clerk had packaged so neatly.

When I was putting my cards back in my wallet he saw my New York state PI ticket in the folder and gave me a scrutinizing look. "You're that Michael Hammer . . . the one who caught that mobster on the old Harris place?"

"Everybody's got to be somebody," I said.

"You were just on television, right before you came in here."

"Come on, no cameras were at Harris'."

"I don't mean there. The police were looking for you."

"What for?"

"Something's happened. They didn't say, but they want you to call any precinct station. You're to ask for . . . a Mr. Holmes?"

"Mr. Watson."

"Yes, that's it. You can use my phone here if you'd like."

I didn't need a phone book. The police and fire department numbers were printed on stickers glued to the phone itself and I dialed the top number. I asked for Homer Watson, gave my name and waited through a patch to a radio in his car. He asked me where I was and he told me to stay in my car until he got there.

Velda saw me coming and jumped out to meet me. She started to say, "There was an announcement about you on the radio . . ."

"I know. It came over TV too. This town has a wild communication system."

"What's it all about?"

"Beats me, but Homer's coming right over. Get back in the car."

Once we were seated she said, "Where have you been?"

"Buying you some candy, kitten." I took the box out of my pocket and handed it to her. Only for one second was there a question on her face, because candy wasn't wrapped like that. There was just that thing about the size and shape and weight of the package that shouted to the world what it was and she tore into the fancy wrappings with nails like a tiger's and yanked it out of the paper. She stared at it for a few seconds, looked at me with the expression that said that this had better not be a joke, then she opened the box.

The kiss was different this time. It was a brand-new experience, a once-in-a-lifetime feeling of fleshly heat and a wild promise of total satisfaction that had waited long enough and now was ready to explode into reality. Her mouth was soft and wet, a hungry lusciousness I didn't want to stop tasting, but did so I could take the ring and slide it on her finger. It was just a little loose, but Velda didn't care at all. Those deep brown eyes caressed mine and got foggy with the tears women get at times like this.

Homer Watson pulled up to snap the moment back to *now.* He hopped out of his car and got in the backseat of mine. "I wish you'd let me know where you are. We've been looking all over for you."

"Hell, I'm not under arrest."

"It could be worse, Hammer. You're under a death threat."

"What else is new?"

"This one's different."

His voice had strange overtones and he kept scanning the streets outside. When he was satisfied that we were clear, he said, "Ugo Ponti is loose. He broke out last night and hasn't been located."

"Come on, Homer. He had a police guard. What happened?"

"A military operation is what happened. We haven't got accurate figures, but from what we put together, eight men came in, subdued the guards, cut the phone lines, herded building personnel into a room and locked it, then got Ugo out of there. They had cutters with them that freed him from the bed frames, clothes to go over his pajamas and they were gone."

"Ugo wouldn't have contacts like that up here," I stated. "I doubt if he could pull that off in his own neighborhood."

"And you'd be right. This wasn't Ugo's show at all."

"Okay, who—"

"The long arm of the Mafia, friend. Lorenzo Ponti was top dog in this area and the local capo decided that he owed his former don a debt of gratitude and arranged for the bust out."

"You sure of this?"

"Absolutely. Two of those hoods were recognized by one of the people they locked up. He told us, but no way will he make that identification official. The cops got the word on the street about it too. Now, the debt's been paid, so the heat is not on you from the mob up here. It's Ugo . . . he's gone completely nuts. All he wants is you, and from the threats he made earlier, he wants your hide."

"What do you want, Homer?"

"I want you to stay alive until we get our hands on that money."

"In other words, you still think I know where it is?"

He didn't answer me, but he didn't have to.

I told him, "Homer, how would anybody know if I had all those billions?"

"You tell me, Hammer," he said.

I let my head move in a slow nod. "I'd have to *show rich* first, wouldn't I?"

His eyes said that I was right.

"My Ford would have to get turned in for a BMW or a Mercedes and I'd move into an apartment on Fifth Avenue." I paused, savoring the picture. "A couple of the agencies could furnish me bodyguards."

Velda let out a chuckle and Homer gave her a concerned look. She said, "You have to get rid of your Hush Puppies and other crepe-soled shoes and carry a smaller gun."

Then it was my turn to laugh. "You know, Homer, the mob doesn't want me. It wants their money, and if there's a chance that I *can* point them to it, I'm safe. If the good old U.S. Department of the Treasury or the IRS or any of those clowns think I have the key, they'll guard me like Fort Knox."

"That leaves Ugo Ponti as the loose cannon. Knowing him, nothing's going to change until he kills you. Or Velda here."

I got that sudden squeeze again. It wrapped itself around my middle, then centered on my side, like a flint arrowhead being pushed into a suppurated wound very slowly, stopping just before the pain got great enough to make you choke on your own breath.

Velda saw my face tighten and knew what was happening.

Homer frowned and said, "What are your plans?"

I knew what I had to do. For too long I had ignored it, but now I knew. I said, "I'm going back to the city, Mr. Watson. There's nothing more I can do here."

"We can run unmarked cars in front and in back of you if you want."

Velda didn't give me a chance to answer. "That will be fine, Mr. Watson." He looked at me and I agreed with a nod.

"I'll call Captain Chambers. Our teams will escort you back to the city limits and his men can cover you back to your apartment. Is that all right with you?"

"Sure." I breathed slowly a few seconds until the pain receded a little. "But isn't all this interdepartmental cooperation a little unusual?"

"Perhaps, but necessary. It makes bookkeeping easier. The prize involved demands it."

"Baloney," I said sourly, "the prize is all that counts."

Velda drove going back, staying a little above the posted speeds like everyone else. The unmarked cars took turns leading our convoy and twice plain vans and a pickup with a camper top joined us to relieve the monotony in case we were being followed. All the cars were in communication by radio and when Pat's men joined us I felt better. The other vehicles seemed to melt away and we made the apartment building without an incident. Bill Raabe was on duty, spotted us, and knew that something was up and didn't ask any questions. When we got upstairs, Velda called Ralph Morgan and told him to get over as fast as he could.

My front door was fireproof, steel faced and solidly bolted and I didn't want an armed guard outside, but Pat insisted and settled for a plainclothesman down in the lobby to keep Bill Raabe company. The patrol cars would make routine stops to check the situation periodically.

Velda wasn't a hysterical female. She was as businesslike as she could get and got into my small arms cabinet and laid out three automatics with full loads at hidden but strategic places around the rooms. I let her play while I slipped into a tub of warm, soothing water and let the pain soften like the dirt on me and got out, dried off and dressed as the good doctor came in.

His face registered pure disgust. There was no small talk until he had gotten all my vital signs down on his pad, a new bandage on me and had a brief conversation with Velda out of my sight. When he came back he said, "You'll live. How long, however, is in your hands. Your general condition is good, but it could have been much better. That wound of yours could erupt at any time. It's right on the edge this minute. I'm not going to preach to you, Mike. It wouldn't do any good. You made me well, for which I thank you, but you'll do nothing for yourself. You haven't got a death wish, have you?"

"Not likely."

"Why don't you retire?"

"From whom, pal? I'm self-employed. I can't quit."

The doctor looked over at Velda and she shrugged in resignation.

"When is this thing going to end?" he asked me.

"When it's over," I said.

Three days went past like a soft dream. I ate, I slept, I watched the weather channel on TV and fell asleep during two movies. Velda whispered around my apartment, keeping things clean and answering the phone. At regular intervals I took what medication she gave me and finally I began to think the doctor had slipped in something to keep me channelled in peaceful paths. There was no company and no noise and on the morning of the fourth day my eyes snapped open to total reality. There was no drug hangover, no pain in my side, and when I touched the bandaged area there was a soreness but nothing more. I was awake, I was alert and I felt great.

Velda had been watching and waiting. I didn't eat in the bed again. I sat up in a chair and had breakfast spread out before me on a small table. The vitamins and the calories were all there, but I wasn't smothered with huge portions. Something had happened to my appetite and the small portions she had doled out were just right.

She had my ring on her finger and I was feeling that being married wouldn't be cutting a hole in my life at all.

That girl was reading my mind again. She deliberately waved the diamond in front of me and smiled. Then she told me to go shave and get cleaned up. Pat had called earlier and would be up to see me in another hour.

Something critical had cropped up.

"This is pure rumor," Pat told me. "It's straight off the streets and not documented at all, but I trust the sources."

"Good news?"

"For you, yeah. The Albany mob that broke Ugo out of the jail hospital found out that he iced his father. The capo of that bunch was tight with old Lorenzo, that's why he did the big favor, but when he got word of Ugo pulling the trigger, he hit the roof. There's a contract out on Ugo like you can't believe. The few old-timers who have their organizations in line are lending a hand and there's no way Ugo is going to get out of this."

"Have they located him yet?"

"Nobody has shown up yet, and his will be one corpse they won't bury under concrete pilings in Jersey. Ugo is going to be a real example."

"He already is, Pat. He's still on the loose."

"The families have tightened the net around New York.

They'd sooner have him dead than controlling that money."

"What money, Pat?" I asked him lightly.

"Knock it off, Mike." He got up from his chair and paced the room twice. "His odds are bad. If the police nail him, he goes to prison. He'll be killed there before they could get him in the chair. Keeping him alive for trial will be harder than trying to locate him."

"What kind of a net have you got out?"

Pat glared out the window. "Every escape route is covered. Local police and the feds are searching the Albany area, but he had all the time in the world to break out of there. We heard the capo in the state capital laid ten grand on him and got him a nondescript car with straight plates, so he had transportation."

"You got the plate numbers?"

"No. That was another rumor from a reliable source. We're waiting for that capo to get sore enough to release the information so we can get an APB out on him."

"They don't do it that way, Pat."

"Maybe this time they might." He turned slowly and looked down at me sipping my second cup of coffee. "Mike, they all know about you. I think they hired historical researchers because Dooley, you and me are pieces of gossip coming out of the sides of mob mouths. I've been called in twice by my superiors to give an explanation of all this, but what do I know? If we were dealing with legitimate business it would be different, but mob money is as elusive as a will-o'-the-wisp. It's there, but it's not there. It's not in use, but the mob business goes on. Nobody seems to know a thing, yet everybody knows all those billions are boxed and stored and a crazy is out there starting up even more trouble for the families."

I said, "Get to your point, Pat."

He hooked the chair with his foot and pulled it under him. "I just want you to tell me the truth, Mike. No fancy speculations. Like Jack Webb used to say, 'Just the facts.' "

"Okay, you got it, Pat."

"Is there really that much money stashed somewhere?"

"Dooley intimated that there was."

"That's not an answer, Mike."

"That's all he told me."

Pat took a deep breath, stared up at the ceiling a moment, then said, "Do you know where it is?"

"No."

Pat was a cop and I didn't fool him a bit. "Do you think you know where it is?"

"I've been studying on that, pal."

"What are your conclusions?"

"So far I haven't gotten to that point. At least we know one thing: nobody else has recovered it. I assume you have alerted every warehouse in the state and have contacted all the hunting clubs to pinpoint cave sites in the Adirondack mountain range, right?"

"Among other efforts. The feds are laying out a barrel of loot to run this thing down. If Ugo turns up in their net it will only be coincidental." His fingers drummed on the arm of the chair. "Tell me, Mike, did you ever figure Dooley for this kind of action?"

"Remember when he ambushed that patrol? He made them think he had a full company behind him."

"We were all young then. That was war."

"So is this, Pat, and it's not over yet."

Pat nodded sagely and said, "I'm restricted to the city, Mike, but you're mobile. Someplace in your head you've schemed something up. You have plans and you are about to start working them out. Am I right?"

"You're close."

"Do I come into this or not?"

"Do you want to?"

"No, not really, but I know I will, so clue me in."

I leaned forward and looked at him. I wasn't about to string him along and jeopardize his job and he knew it. We were back on hostile ground facing an armed enemy who had more troops than we did and who could disappear into the civilized bushes of a city without a trace.

I said, "Stick by your phone, Pat. I'll call at the right time."

New York had turned grey again. There was a chill to the wind that blew from the Hudson River and dust devils rose from the sidewalks and blew in your face so you could actually taste what the city was like. It was nasty and indigestible. There was nothing in common with the smell that loped around the soft rises of the mountains. There, you could smell the trees and the green things and windows didn't vibrate from the street noises and exhaust emissions followed the thruway and didn't intrude on the countryside. Acid rain touched the pines on the mountain peaks, but that was a disorder born in industrial cities far from the mellow foliage of the real New York, the part they call the North Country now.

Leaving the city without a tail was no trouble. Just to be sure, I doubled my little tricks and got on the New York Thruway with nobody in sight. At the restaurant area by the Middletown cutoff we pulled into the parking lot and sat there, surveying the traffic. Only two cars stopped, each one with big families. One had Pennsylvania plates and the other Ontario.

So far it had been a clean run. We locked the car, throwing an old khaki jacket over the two cellular phones on the seat. There was no more demand for CB radios. Personal telephones were the big deal for vandals. Then we went inside and got a booth where we had a clear vision of traffic on Route 87.

Over a bowl of hot oatmeal Velda said, "When do you tell me what's going on?"

"We're going to find the money, doll."

"And what are you going to do with it?"

"Nothing. I'm just going to find it."

"Do you know where it is?"

I grinned at her. "I think so." Her eyes narrowed and she waited for me to tell her. I shook my head. "You wouldn't want to know, honey."

"Why not?"

"Too many bats."

Her mouth twitched and she said sharply, "Stop it, Mike." Then her eyes grew grimmer for an instant. "You *are* going back to Harris' cave again, aren't you?"

"Dooley wasn't fooling about those numbers, kitten. He knew what he was doing."

"That cave was saturated with experts and they didn't find a thing!"

"They weren't the right kind of experts," I told her. "They only thought they were doing a clever search job."

"What did they miss?"

"Latitude and longitude gives you an exact location. Out on the ocean you can locate the exact spot within a couple of feet with regular loran equipment. You can give me a number and I can run right to the spot . . . if I know how to use the equipment."

"But you *gave* them the numbers you found on Dooley's boat."

"I didn't tell them what Dooley had told me, though. He had changed the signs so the arrows pointed in the wrong direction. Those loran numbers crossed in the middle of the big cave. Nothing was there at all. In fact, the spot wasn't even in the middle of the cave, but down toward one end."

"How did you find that out? You didn't have any equipment with you."

"An offhand remark one of the feds made who did have the equipment. He thought the whole business was a red herring dreamed up by a loony who had a big gripe against the government."

"But *you* don't think so, do you, Mike?"

"I believe Dooley, kid."

"Then let's do it."

We made two stops in the Albany area before I drove to a farm equipment place outside of town. I told the manager I wanted to rent a small backhoe and a pick and shovel combo to do some digging on property I just bought. I told him it was a simple job I could handle myself if he showed me how to run the backhoe. It wasn't too far off what I had used a few times in the army, so the lessons were quick and I signed the papers for the stuff. He hooked a trailer hitch to the rear of my car, loaded the backhoe on a trailer and slid the trailer hitch on the ball then waved me off.

Velda was giving me another of those "who *are* you" looks again. She said, "Mike, I don't believe you. Where did you learn about this machinery?"

"I didn't know you were such a nurse, either," I said.

"We've been out in the field together before."

"Not like this. And we were younger then."

"Are we smarter?" she asked me.

"If we're not, we're in trouble."

Getting to Harris' property now was no problem. All

the recent traffic had widened the opening of the driveway, crushing down the weeds that almost obscured it earlier. I swung wide, turned up the road, dropped the transmission into low range. Those many cars had made the road smoother, so hauling the backhoe wasn't much trouble at all. I crept by the see-through slash in the trees, passed the old wrecked Mack truck and came out on the plateau of the property.

The residue from a couple of hundred official visitors was plain. Cigarette wrappers were all over the place, with soda cans and quick food bags making it look like a sloppy camper's picnic area.

I drove up to the semi-hidden opening to the cave, lowered the wheel ramps on the trailer, started up the backhoe and drove it off. While I flipped on the lights and went into the cave, Velda drove the car into the nearest grove of trees and joined me in that vast empty dome that was a bootlegger's perfect warehouse.

She hopped up beside me and clung to my neck as I drove across the dirt floor. Too many feet had softened the crust and the dust hung thick in the air. I had thought this could happen, so brought a couple of plastic filters that we slipped over our heads. Breathing became a little better then.

I started where the numbers intersected, fifty feet back from the rear of the wall. The pile of rubble Slateman said had come from the roof lay straight ahead, looking for all the world like it had been pushed there to get it out of the way of the trucks.

But Slateman was wrong. None of that rubble had come down from the ceiling. The scarring above was minimal compared to the pile below. I touched the controls and dropped the scoop, and while Velda stepped down to watch the operation, I started digging into the seemingly immovable heap of stone.

Only at first was it difficult, most of it due to my inefficiency with the scoop, but once I had the routine down it became faster. In thirty minutes the rubble had been parted and the scoop was digging in loose, pebbly material and I knew I was almost there. I lifted the scoop and left the engine running with the lights blazing and took the pickax and began hacking at the indentation.

Velda said, "You're through, Mike. There's nothing back there."

"Oh, there's something back there, all right," I told her through labored breaths. I used the shovel, scraping the dirt away until the hole was wide enough for the two of us to walk through without scraping.

You could hear them now. They made funny noises at being disturbed, tiny sounds and noise like the beating of wings. Velda looked at me, her eyes wide, holding back from entering the hole in the wall.

"They're bats, kitten. Millions of bats. They're bottled up in here guarding eighty-nine billion dollars."

"How do they get out?" There was a shudder in her voice.

"Someplace there's an opening. It's probably well concealed and you'd only spot it when the bats exit the area. But we know it's there and *we* know how to get back in here again." I took her arm and gave her a tug. She didn't move. I pushed a little harder and she took a reluctant step.

"Mike . . ."

"What?"

"They don't *really* get caught in your hair, do they?"

"You should know better," I reminded her. "They

have the best radar system in the world. They won't even touch you."

Velda nodded. She believed me. She knew it was the truth, but her steps were still forced.

The fierce light from the backhoe's floods made it seem like the opening of an ancient tomb. There was a smell of age, and the magnificence of the gigantic casket that rose six cartons high and fifty feet wide, diminishing into the darkness of the hole beyond it, made us feel tiny in comparison.

I took out my pocket knife and went to the nearest carton and slit an opening in its side, finally making a door that revealed the packets of green inside. I pulled out a dozen wrapped bundles of hundreds, counted out a certain amount and put the remainder back in the carton.

Velda watched carefully and said, "What's that for?"

"Office expenses. This was a job, remember? Okay, I'm paying us."

"How much?"

"Enough to pay for your ring, our salaries and Uncle Sam his taxes."

"How are you going to declare it?"

"As a cash deal. No explanations. Our client was anonymous. We've had plenty of clients like that."

"Aren't you going to look in the other cartons?"

"Nope. We know what's there. Eighty-nine billion dollars less our share. Someplace in there is a pile of gold, industrial securities . . . all that good stuff, but who needs to count? We'll never get to use it, but we know where it is and we'll never tell. But there are those who will know we found it. They can't do anything about it without leaving themselves open to the law. They'll figure we arranged for that to happen."

She was beginning to smile now. It was like that old song, "I've Got Plenty of Nothing."

I said, "Don't laugh, kitten. Do you know what we'll really have for sure?"

"No, tell me."

"The greatest credit rating in the world. We could go to Vegas and have a ball in the casinos and they'd give us anything we wanted."

"Can't we just stay at home and work the way we used to?"

This time I laughed. "Absolutely, kitten. I was only kidding."

Covering up the entrance wasn't going to be as easy as opening it. Dooley had done a capable job, but he had more time to do it. There was no telling who would come in here now and spot what I had done. I looked over the area carefully, noting the shape of the ledge that was like a lintel over the hole I had dug. There was enough loosely packed rock there to solve the whole situation if it could be brought down.

Velda came up beside me. The thought of the bats inside kept her right by my side. "What's the problem?"

"I need a demolition man," I said. "That would solve this one."

Her mind started doing some mental gymnastics. "Mike . . . under the seat in your car . . ."

I exploded with a "Damn!" and ran across the cave to the entrance. I saw where she had parked the Ford and yanked the door open. It took a minute to pull out that packet of explosive that was supposed to blow us to jelly. When I got back to the backhoe Velda was standing between the headlights, flattened against the radiator.

To the wires on the charge I added another thirty feet from a roll in the tool box on the backhoe. I placed that little oblong package of destruction against the opening, protected ourselves behind the backhoe's battery and the blast banged against our eardrums.

But it did the job. The opening was sealed. It took another hour to get the exterior rubble back in place and to drive over the area enough to pack it down. When I let the lights run over it, the place looked pretty much like it did before.

It took another hour to get the backhoe on the trailer and hooked up, then we started back down the mountain again.

And then that rain with the frosty breath behind it started misting up the windshield. I turned on the wipers and flipped on the lights. The dark was coming in fast and the visibility was getting sour. I touched the brakes, but the ground that had been packed so tight had gotten slippery with the rain and the backhoe trailer didn't have a brake hookup and was a deadly crusher in back of us.

I angled the car to the right, getting off the downhill slope and came to a stop. Velda shot me a concerned glance and said, "What do we do now?"

I opened the door and slipped out. "We leave that piece of equipment right here. No way I could make it down to the highway with that thing. We can bring it back another day."

"Need a hand?"

"No. Just sit tight."

Getting the trailer unhitched was easy enough. Getting down the hill was another story. The wind had picked up and blew the foliage with it, making it brush against the car, distorting our visibility. The ground wasn't soaking up the water at all, letting it flow down the tire tracks, eliminating the car's traction.

Beside me, Velda said nothing and breathed heavily.

Twice I hit the brakes, the wheels locked, but we didn't stop. Luckily we hit a patch of gravel that gave the tires a bite and we slowed down. I dumped the transmission into low and let the engine brake as well as the wheels. I could feel the car still picking up speed, little by little. If it got out of hand I'd be driving a couple of tons of momentum right down a black alley.

And there it was back again, the *BLACK ALLEY*. Before it was just me. Now Velda was riding into it too.

There was a harsh crunching sound and branches slashed against the window and the car jerked and slowed. The wind-driven brush had gotten caught under the wheels and the drag was another braking effect.

"How far are we from the road, Mike?"

"A half mile, maybe."

"Would it be better to walk?"

"Let's push it as far as we can. At least we're dry. If a tree comes down there's a roof over us." I touched the gas pedal and we rocked over the blown underbrush, seemed to stall out at the top, then went over the peak and gained forward momentum. The low gear was holding us in the tire ruts, but the minute the speed picked up, the car started fishtailing toward the trees on either side. It seemed like almost a sure thing that we were going to get wrapped around the trunk of a pine, then the roadbed firmed out and the tire treads bit in again and we had traction enough to move and steer.

Both of us heard the sound of heavy truck traffic and knew we were near the paved county road. The tension left us like the sudden unwinding of a spring. Then the road was clear and before I pulled out on the pavement Velda looked at me, and I said, "And you wanted to walk."

"Why do you make everything seem so easy?" she chided me.

I grinned at her, then sat there until another set of headlights swept past us. The rain was heavier now, angling down with a determined viciousness. There was a glow down the road and I waited for that to turn to headlights and when the red taillights went by I steered onto the asphalt.

Two cars passed on the other side of the road followed by a logging truck. A pickup passed us with a patched-top convertible right behind it. Velda wanted to know where all the traffic was coming from on a backwoods road and all I could think of was a possible traffic tie-up on the major highway. I turned on the radio, found the local channel, but there were no accident reports going out. I did pick up a weather station that said an unusual frontal system was bringing in heavy rains and winds and that driving was going to be hazardous.

Great.

I slowed down, squinting through the windshield. Both wipers were going at full speed but the road ahead was a dark, wet blur. The lights from three cars crept up on me until I was the leader in the parade and when the closest one leaned on his horn to get me to speed it up I shook my head at his idiocy and stayed at my own speed. The driver gave in to his impatience, passed me in a shower of spray, almost lost it when he straightened out and kept on going until he was lost in the darkness. The other two cars behind me got the message and stayed right where they were.

Up ahead the lights from a small city put a muted glow in the sky and when we got to a road sign that indicated a motel not far ahead, I turned at the intersection, drove to the tight little cluster of old-fashioned cabins and stopped at the office.

An old man was watching TV and looked up, surprised, when I opened the door. I said, "You have any vacancies?"

It was as if I told him a joke. "That's all I have, mister. The summer season's over and until the snows hit, nobody is going to be here at all."

"How come you're minding the store?"

"If you knew my wife you wouldn't ask that. At least here I have my own TV. Want a cabin?"

"I'm not going any further in this weather."

"Take number four. That one don't leak and it's right beside the hot water tank." He looked out the window at my car. "Just you and your wife. No pets."

I said, "No pets." There wasn't much sense telling him we weren't married yet. I wanted to stay close to Velda. Too much was happening to take any chances of her getting ambushed. The possibility of Ugo getting a lead on us was remote at this point and I wanted to keep it that way.

I took the key, went back to the car and drove up to the fourth cabin, got the bags out of the backseat and ran for the porch. When we got inside and I turned the lights on I felt like a homesteader. We were back a couple of centuries into log cabin living with modern conveniences, a fireplace with cut oak ready to burn, two lounge chairs facing it and, like a lovely invitation, a pair of double beds with golden maple frames.

Velda made no suggestion. She wore a little self-satisfied smile that was telling me the future was right ahead and for the time being she would play the game. We were in a bind and she wouldn't make it worse with the things an engaged woman can do to a man when the chips were down like this. She showered, put on another one of those wild jump suits that meant she was ready to move out in a hurry if we had to, then jumped into bed.

I took the lounge chair. My .45 in the shoulder holster I draped over the back of the small chair, took the inch shorter Combat Commander and tucked it in the cushion beside me, then tilted the back toward the wall and put my feet up.

One thing, I wasn't expecting to fall asleep.

But I did.

There are some things you simply can't control. Snoring. Falling asleep. While I was thinking it dropped on me like a blanket.

It wasn't the feel of cold metal at my temple that brought me awake. It was the light from the lamp beside my chair. It was dull and yellow, but lit the room enough so I could see Velda in the bed, a tight gag wound around her mouth, her hands and feet cinched by strips of tape. There was a contusion on the left side of her forehead from where she had been knocked unconscious while she slept.

She wasn't unconscious now. Her eyes were wide open, hatred and fear spilling out of them at the same time, staring at the person holding the gun to my head.

I turned just enough to recognize who it was and said, "Nice trick, Ugo."

"No trick," he replied. "I'm just smarter than you."

There are times when there is nothing to say. I watched Ugo walk up beside me, the nose of his gun still against my head. I could see just enough of him to catch his smirk at my gun slung over the chair. The way I was slumped in the lounger meant it would take at least three seconds to get on my feet under the best of conditions, which would be two seconds too long. He could put a half dozen shots in me without any kind of trouble in that time span.

All I could do was sit quietly and play the hand out. As far as he was concerned I was no more than cold meat and so was Velda. What he didn't know was that I had on body armor too and a .45 Combat Commander where I might get a chance to use it. He kept thinking that I was a dummy for letting my piece get so far away from me.

I had to get him talking, enough so that the .45 in the leather holster would keep him focused in on that, letting him enjoy the moment. I said, "You didn't know we were coming here, Ugo."

"Didn't have to. I was behind you all the way."

I let an amazed expression cross my face. It was forced, but he didn't know that.

"You think I didn't know you'd come back to Harris' place? Man, that Dooley wouldn't go to all that trouble of stashing the families' money without leaving a roadmap. It's right up there on that mountain."

The hatred in Velda's eyes had given way to resignation—utter, hopeless resignation. This time I could read her mind. We were so close. She had her big ring, we had a license to marry. One more day and the union would have been solidified. All she knew was that we didn't have that one more day. Briefly, the hatred came back, then sank down in despair again.

"The feds had teams of experts up there. They didn't find a thing," I told him. I tried to keep a flutter in my voice.

"So they didn't look in the right place, did they?"

"They looked everywhere. Go check it out."

"I don't have to. You did it for me. You know where Dooley hid it all. That's why you took that digger up there and you found it too. Don't give me any crap about not knowing where it was. Those numbers came together right inside that cave. So he had to bury it right there." He paused and grinned. "Now that was pretty smart, digging a hole in a cave."

Ugo Ponti decided to move a little so he could see me better and when he moved I did too, just enough to position my hand so I could make a grab for the rod at my side. He raised the gun in his hand, a short-barrelled .38. If I took a head shot I'd be out of it instantly, so if he decided to shoot I was hoping I would be hit in the chest. Knowing Ugo's mentality, I didn't expect him to try for a fast kill. He'd want to see me hurting before he tagged me for good. He'd want Velda to see it too before he laid one on her.

"How'd you get in here, Ugo?"

The question seemed to insult him. We both knew I would have heard the door opening if he had picked the lock. Hell, I felt the change of temperature in the room when I first woke up and knew how he'd gotten in.

He answered me anyway. "Hammer, I was doing window jobs with the edge of a carborundum sharpening stone when I was a kid. I got class now. I used a real glass-cutting tool, a suction cup and a small tap to break out a hole in the window. Then I reached in and opened the lock. You should know about those things. You've done the same thing yourself plenty of times."

"Why, Ugo?" I asked him. "This won't get you anyplace. The local soldiers that broke you out up here have a contract on you already."

"When I get that money I'll buy their soldiers. But you, Hammer . . . you I'm going to kill. You won't die too fast. You'll have time to see me put one in your girlfriend and she won't die too fast either. You might even have enough time to say good-bye to each other. How do you like that?"

As long as he was standing in front of me I hadn't taken my eyes off him. I was riveted on his face, his mouth and his eyes. I didn't look at the gun at all. Then suddenly my head moved, my eyes widened as I looked at Velda and he half turned to see what had happened behind his back and in that instant of time when situations change he realized that it was a ruse and he screamed with rage and let a shot go at me that slammed me back into the recliner, but the shot I snapped off caught him square in the sternum and he went down on his back, the .38 clattering from his hand.

The one that had hit me was like a monstrous blow from a giant's fist and for a few seconds I couldn't get my breath. I slammed the footrest down and half stood up. The slug had given me one violent punch, but it hadn't pierced the weave of modern technology.

Nor had my .45 destroyed Ugo. He was looking at me, the daze coming out of his eyes to let sheer amazement show through. I walked over and picked up his gun and shoved it in my belt.

He was getting his breath back now.

I grinned and shot him a little lower down in the chest. His eyes bugged out and he gave a couple of violent jerks.

Velda was watching the tableau unfold, her eyes hardly believing what she saw. I walked over and pulled the tape off her arms and legs, letting her handle the muffling gags.

The pain hadn't started on Ugo yet. It would be another minute or two before the brutal impact of the .45 round against his rib cage would make the agony sweep up like engulfing fire. I said, "That body armor only stops the penetration, kid. This rod of mine is loaded with standard army cap and ball ammo, nice soft lead slugs that won't get inside you but will break every bone you have. You'll be screaming to die after the sixth shot and you'll remember all the reasons this is coming at you."

I didn't have to emphasize it. He knew I was going

to do it and the dread was plain in the expression on his face.

"Mike . . ." She said it very softly.

I frowned, watching her.

"Don't end it for us."

You could count the seconds going past while I let it all run through my mind. When I looked down at Ugo I knew the pain was almost there so I told him very calmly, "It was a wild-goose chase, Ugo. There was no money. There never was any money at all. The big bosses in the family had blown it. They never said why or how, but they didn't want to go down at the hands of their kids. That's why they dreamed up this wild story. Dooley just faked it out for them and I was part of that fake. No money, Ugo. No big crime family of your own. But the contract is still out on you and it won't go away."

His breath was coming in wheezes, but he was understanding me.

"I'm taking you back to the city with us. I can drop you with some police who won't let the word go out that you're in custody. If you play your cards right you might get put in a safe cell where you'll stay alive for eighty or ninety years. Or I can drop you off outside a certain storefront in Manhattan where the club members will be happy to boil you in oil while they watch."

I got three pairs of handcuffs out of the car and snapped them on Ugo Ponti. He fit on the floor beside the backseat making pitiful sounds as he thought over his options. Halfway back to New York he told me where he preferred to go. I picked up the cellular phone, called Pat and made arrangements for the transfer.

It was all done very neatly.

In the east it was getting light, a soft warmth trying to get through the cold, damp mist.

Velda said, "Where do we go from here?"

I knew she wanted to go park outside the courthouse until the judge got there. Women are like that.

"Your choice, kitten," I told her. Then I turned and threw up. She looked at my face and I knew I was pale. My knees were shaky and there was a blaze in my chest where Ugo's slug had hit me. But the black alley wasn't there this time.

"I'm taking you home, Mike. I'm calling Ralph Morgan and you're going to do what he says as long as he wants."

I wiped my mouth. "I thought you wanted to get married."

"That will come," she told me.

"Then let's go home," I said.